THE ROAD THROUGH SAN JUDAS

★

ROBERT FRAGA

The Road Through San Judas
Robert Fraga
© 2019 PM Press.
All rights reserved. No part of this book may be transmitted by any means
without permission in writing from the publisher.

ISBN: 978-1-62963-649-8
Library of Congress Control Number: 2018949083

Cover image by Gavin Snider
Cover by John Yates / www.stealworks.com
Interior design by briandesign

10 9 8 7 6 5 4 3 2 1

PM Press
PO Box 23912
Oakland, CA 94623
www.pmpress.org

Printed in the USA.

WHY THIS BOOK AND WHY NOW?

This book grew out of a stint working as a volunteer on a construction project designed to provide affordable and environmentally sensitive insulation for a humble restaurant located to the west of Ciudad Juárez in the north of Mexico. The work on its insulation is the focus of the first chapter of the book. On my last day on the job, I met the intrepid priest on whom my character Father Joe is loosely based. With his allies, this man struggled month after month to save the homes of his parishioners from being destroyed by a rich and avaricious family of land developers.

Ultimately wealth and influence prevailed, but this book is a testament to the valor of the combatants. Recording their struggle is, I feel, their historical and literary victory.

FROM THE JOURNAL
OF A VOLUNTEER

To the north lay Texas and New Mexico. Those states lay beyond the wall separating Old Mexico from the U.S.

In the foreground: a grid of unpaved streets and what looked like sheds. People actually lived in these sheds.

Wood pallet fences enclosed dust-caked yards. Even the gates were made of wood pallets taken from the loading docks of American-owned factories strung along the border. Past the shell of an abandoned school bus, its white paint peeling, its wheels half-buried in sand, we looked across the plain of Anapra, beyond a razor-thin sliver of New Mexico, to the Franklin Mountains of West Texas. This was to be our home for the next two weeks. *This* was one of the poorest neighborhoods of Ciudad Juárez. Its horizontality was punctured irregularly by eucalyptus and scrub oak. The trees rose like eruptions from the desert below.

To the west lay a soccer pitch. No grass, just sand. Just like the rest of Anapra. The local teams, kitted out in white shorts and red and blue shirts, played on Sundays. They yelled and raised sprays of dust as they kicked the ball back and forth across the sand. Beyond the pitch rose a stone-ribbed butte. As flat as Anapra itself but higher, one hundred feet above the *colonia*. This was the mesa where it stood: San Judas, the barrio that is the focus of this book, a region buffeted by strong winds that we would experience later during our stay.

To the east, there was nothing to see. That side of the house was built of rock and cement. To the south, it abutted a north facing hill. During the day, light seeped through clerestory windows above a sink and kitchen counters. Our (indoor) bathroom lay just to the west of the dormitory space. There were hot-water showers—a luxury in Anapra—and ordinary sinks, but the toilets were dry pits. After a dump or a leak, we would take a tin can that stood beside each of the toilets and toss a mixture of sand and lime down the hole. A series of stick-figure graphics, captioned in Spanish (*Si lo usas, usalo bi*en) and tacked to the wall, illustrated the dos and don'ts of dry toilet etiquette.

This would be our home for the next two weeks. Casa Emaus: an elongated one-room building, partitioned at both ends into smaller cubicles, where we slept amidst a jumble of shelving units. The whole building was tucked into a hillside. On the north side—the side that faced the U.S.—a concrete porch ran the length of the house. The ridgepole, supported by square sectioned brick columns, was home to a pair of sparrows. There the birds had built a nest under the corrugated steel roof. We shared our home with birds. Amicably: no territorial squabbles; no dispute over space. The sparrows had as much right to be there as we did. The birds darted in and out of their nest. They seemed to shoot us quizzical looks when they alighted on their aerie. Were they asking themselves what the hell we were doing there? At night, we stood on the porch and watched the car lights stream silently along the I-10 in Texas. On our side of the border—on our side of the wall—we could hear the nonstop barking of dogs. We could smell the roasted *elotes*, ears of corn. Peddlers who roamed the streets sold them from their pushcarts.

The sparrows were asking the right question: What *were* we doing there? Not that there were many of us. For the entire two weeks, there were only our group leader—Alfred von Bachmayr, commonly called "Von"—an American despite his aristocratic German name, José Bernal—a construction worker from California, two volunteers—myself and a young woman whose name was Erin Campbell, and two old hands— Dean Coil and Gary Aitkin. A total of six.

Erin, a pixie blonde from a Catholic convent in eastern Kentucky, was a skilled and experienced builder. Very handy with construction tools was she. So were Dean and Gary. Dean Coil had the physique and complexion of a Viking. He hailed from Minnesota and was about to marry and settle down in Chihuahua. His second marriage, this one was to a local woman who worked as the principal of a Chihuahua school. He was a kind of on-site manager of the project and the only one of us who actually lived in Mexico.

José Bernal was a dark-skinned, lean man. His eyes were grey, almost colorless. People first meeting José sometimes thought that he suffered from glaucoma. His friends had nicknamed him Wolf Eyes, Ojos del Lobo. He was a Mexican American, a man in his thirties, who had been born in Chiapas, in the south of Mexico. His father, a peasant farmer, had gone bankrupt and migrated north. So José had grown up in the barrio of San Judas, where we were living. Somehow the family had scraped together the money to send him to high school and college. He came back regularly to Mexico, although he worked mostly on construction projects in California and other Western states.

Gary Aitkin, the last to show up, had the body and coloring of a greyhound, a two-legged greyhound at that, thin to the point of emaciation and bushy bearded. He had come by bus from Guatemala where he had wintered, holed up on a sailboat. Now he was en route back to his home in Montana. Anapra was like the halfway point on his homeward journey. Gary Aitkin invariably shortened our group leader's last name to Von. Other volunteers from Santa Fe and Las Cruces worked with us but not for the duration of the project. In addition, we had two Mexican laborers. These guys were actually paid.

Paid for what? Volunteering for what? Our job was to do a straw wrap of a cinderblock building. Von reckoned packing straw against the cinder blocks to be an ecologically sensitive and inexpensive way to insulate the building against summer's heat and the cold of winter. Almost all the materials were secured locally: Straw from farms to the east of Juárez. Wood pallets from factories and markets of the city itself. The restaurant that the building housed was scheduled to open the day after our arrival.

Von Bachmayr was an architect whose passion was sustainable building. A graduate of the University of Colorado, he once built a house for an eighty-four-year-old great grandmother living on a Navajo reservation in New Mexico. Von's volunteers erected a straw bale house for the woman in two weeks. She now had—for the first time in her life—electricity generated by a photovoltaic array and a roof cistern to catch water for her and, if the rains were plentiful, for her sheep.

The straw wrap was not the first of von Bachmayr's projects in Ciudad Juárez: three years earlier he had directed a project to build a house from shipping pallets. This was similar in concept to what we would be doing in 2008. Land for the earlier project had been secured by a priest of the

Columban Order: Father Joe Borelli, a man who plays a crucial role in the story of San Judas.

Von's group was called the World Hands Project. It was an offshoot of Builders Without Borders (BWB), an organization he cofounded in 2002. The architect's interest lay in straw bale structures like the one he had built on the Navajo reservation, but he had also been exploring ways to make trusses out of wood pallets. His work with BWB brought him to the attention of a missionary group called Casa de la Cruz. This group was involved in constructing low-cost housing along the U.S.-Mexican border. This was how Von Bachmayr came to Ciudad Juárez.

A raucous choir of cocks woke us up that first day. To get to the worksite, we squeezed into Alfred's truck, a Toyota with a topper over its bed. To thwart thieves, we carried our tools back and forth between the worksite and Casa Emaus, hauling heavy chests and electric saws and a blue plastic water canteen down from the house to the alley where the van was parked. At the end of the day, we repeated the procedure in reverse. The routine never varied, even in its details, step by step, Monday through Friday. More often than not, on the drive itself I sat in the rear, my feet dangling over the lowered tailgate of the truck, with the rocks and the sand of the side streets, then the macadam of the main highway through Anapra, slipping beneath them. We bounced over the speed bumps, gripping every available protuberance of the Toyota for fear of being pitched out into the road. These kamikaze runs would have been illegal north of the border. In Anapra, it was the only way to commute if we were to avoid a time- and fuel-wasting shuttle service. Our destination lay half a mile away. The restaurant stood at the northwest corner of a yard where we parked and unloaded the van. And that was what we did, day after day: unpacking in the morning, loading up in the evening. Nothing of value was ever left at the worksite, not even if it could be locked up. Anapra was a very, very poor neighborhood.

The last day in March and the first of our workdays saw the inauguration of the restaurant. For the grand opening, a festive meal of chicken cordon bleu was prepared. While we did our thing outside, the three women proprietors of Las Abejas (The Bees) kept buzzing round the kitchen. The women's cooperative that ran Las Abejas was the creation of two ex-nuns, Elvia Villalobos and Lina Sarlat. They called their own minuscule operation Las Hormigas (The Ants).

Villalobos and Sarlat had come to Anapra in 2004. Times were bad. The previous ten years saw hundreds of women murdered in Ciudad Juárez. Few of these crimes were solved to anyone's satisfaction. Amnesty International did a study of what came to be known as the femicides of Juárez and found that at least 137 of the female victims had been murdered by sexual predators.

"We have found this pattern repeated over and over again," said Sarlat. "The men expect their women to be at home ironing and cleaning and cooking. They get jealous and accuse them of having other men. Then they beat them or kill them."

After their arrival in Anapra, Sarlat and Villalobos, then in their forties, opened a counseling center. With U.S. assistance, they schooled children who were thought to be at risk. Another of their projects was to help women in Anapra set up a transport cooperative to provide a commuter service into downtown Juárez where food prices were cheaper. This ship quickly foundered on the shoal of macho pride: male bus drivers stopped the unwanted competition. Next came a spinoff project, a sort of meals-on-wheels venture. Women sold meals out of their van: beef and chili stew with beans and tortillas for the equivalent of $1.80. Then—and this is where we came in—the Women's collective restaurant: Las Abejas. The ex-nuns persuaded three enterprising women to open a restaurant on the highway passing through Anapra.

While the three cooks buzzed around the kitchen, our team erected an awning to protect us from the sun. The material used was a pair of blue tarps. Bales of straw, to be used later for the insulation, lay stacked against the wall that separated the restaurant compound from the neighbor's property to the west. The straw came from a feedlot where cattle were fattened up for sale in the U.S. A jumble of pallets, soon to be sawed up and reconfigured as trusses, lay a few feet away. We improvised a workbench under the shade of the tarps. It was supported by bales of straw. Then lunchtime. But first a blessing on the restaurant by Padre Pablo, an elderly American priest with wispy white hair. He was Father Joe's replacement in Anapra. (*Why* Father Joe was replaced figures in our story.) Padre Pablo was the guest of honor at the meal that Las Abejas whipped up. Lina Sarlat and Elvia Villalobos were rarely at the worksite, but they came for the opening ceremony. Padre Pablo sprinkled holy water with a sprig of laurel, and we trooped into the restaurant for the chicken feast. There were about fifteen invitees, children and adults, not including our group. That filled up the restaurant. Las Abejas was small: a whitewashed room with four round tables, each with three or four white plastic chairs. The windows were framed with translucent orange curtains, knotted to shorten them so that they hung above the window sills. Yellow balloons floated in one corner of the room to mark the festive nature of the occasion.

After lunch, we went back to work, sawing up pallets and assembling trusses. Von Bachmayr is a pioneer in using discarded pallets as a building material for roofs. He found that the pallets could be taken apart with a reciprocating saw without damaging the individual pallet boards. Erin and Gary then reassembled the pallets as trusses on a jig installed under the shade of the tarps. Dean penciled lines on the jig to indicate the position of the pallet boards, which were then aligned, glued, and clamped to the rails of the jig.

★

Our Mexican workers—Evaristo and Manny—were experienced at this sort of work. They were unfailingly cheerful, showing up at the worksite early in the morning, day after day, ready to work.

I spent most of my time with Evaristo, a ruddy-complexioned, stocky man. Evaristo was energetic. He was also diabetic. He never ceased to smile and offer encouragement to the less gifted among us. Evaristo had worked for Von Bachmayr before. What improvement I made in my Spanish I owe to him.

Manny was the crew's Lothario, a rakish man with a pencil-thin mustache. He was married, but his wife was some place down south very far from Ciudad Juárez. Manny had custody of their daughter—unaccountably—but he was still lonely. He kept company with a local woman whom he sought to impress. Why he chose to do it this way, Quetzalcoatl only knows, but day after day he badgered me to translate Spanish expressions into French. These were generally expressions like "I love you." Presumably English did not measure up as a language of love, and French had a romantic reputation. Manny worked hard to get the pronunciation down right. And if he didn't quite pull it off, so what? Morning after morning, he would show up looking pleased with himself and satisfied. He attributed his success to my translations and kept asking for more.

Day 2: even in the Spartan living conditions at Casa Emaus, we slept like the dead after our first day's exertions. April Fool's Day we awoke with the cock-a-doodle-dos. But this morning, before bouncing over Anapra's speed bumps back to the worksite, we began the day with a visit to a clinic that Von Bachmayr had designed and built two years before.

Literally next door to Casa Emaus, Santo Nino Clinica Guadalupana was run by a religious order called the Sisters of Charity. Their facility existed before Von improved it, but that facility—built of concrete blocks and roofed with corrugated steel—was habitable only in the mildest of weather.

What Von Bachmayr did was to sink a new foundation made of tires—ordinary, tread-bare tires. This was a technique employed by other architects building in communities strapped for cash. Von's team added two straw bale extensions to the existing structure. Then they coiffed the whole with a pallet truss roof. The clinic specialized in treating children with neurological disorders. The incidence of these problems—described as unusually high in the border region between Mexico and the U.S.—may be tied to working conditions in the maquilas. The Sisters of Charity bathe children in a whirlpool tub. During our visit, we watched a nurse's assistant prepping one little girl for her bath. She was dressed in a diaper and a rust-red sweater. She could not walk. Her legs were like fleshy spindles. Ready to support her weight was a mesh net dangling from the end of a rod.

The clinic walls were painted like those in houses by the Mexican architect Luis Barragán: sienna and turquoise, lemon and grey and grapefruit. They bore crosses and crude renderings of religious subjects, even a traditional depiction of the Virgin Mary, and the word "God" in English—the nuns are North American—above a swollen brace of dove's wings. A series of sketches offered advice to mothers with disabled children. They reminded me of the instructions at Casa Emaus on how to use a dry toilet: there were exercises on how to strengthen their crippled kids' limbs and bodies. Another panel—slicker, more professionally executed, against a pale purple background—illustrated the development of a fetus from inception to birth. Below the panel, someone had written instructions on nursing: five steps, each one with an accompanying photograph.

Finally, on to the worksite, more trusses, more studs. For volunteers, we worked with lightning speed. We hauled the trusses up to the roof and nailed them in place. Studs were positioned on the south and east walls of the restaurant. The west wall was flush with the neighbor's property and would not be insulated. The north wall, fronting the road, would be dealt with a week later. But on two sides, at least, the ribs were in place to gird the straw and mud mixture we used for insulation. One mishap—there were a few in the two weeks of the project—a volunteer from Santa Fe whacked her thumb with a hammer. For the next couple of days she spun a fat white bandage round the injured digit. She even carried her arm briefly in a sling.

That evening, after our return to Casa Emaus, we walked through the backstreets of Anapra to Evaristo's grocery store. This was one of many *abarrotes* in our neighborhood. Evaristo's store was special in two respects: he sold plants in pots and cardboard containers and plastic pails, all lined up neatly in a tiny yard in front of the store. And he was expanding: a stone and cinder block wing was going up just to the right of the door of the store. Beyond that door, his wife Lara sold eggs and long preservation milk, bottled water, food in plastic wrappers, and tinfoil-wrapped sweets stored in glass canisters. Evaristo needed the space. It was unclear where the family slept in this one-room grocery store/house. Maybe under a small, wall-mounted TV that loomed over the counter?

A woman named Gloria supplied our meals. She lived three blocks to the west of Casa Emaus and contracted out the preparation of our *frijoles y arroz*. Sometimes this came with *molé* and chicken. The woman who did the actual cooking lived over the cusp of a hill in the opposite direction. Each night a couple of us would trudge off over the hill to collect our supper, which came in large stainless steel pots. We would clean and return the pots the following day for our cook to fill them up again. This was how we handled our meals, with only a few breaks in what became a monotonous diet. Every morning at Las Abeyas, the women would offer us freshly squeezed orange juice. That was a treat, but one that Evaristo, a diabetic, should have resisted. We learned later that he had to increase his medication as a result of guzzling too much *jugo de naranja.*

One night Gloria paid us a visit to Casa Emaus. She was a small, chunky woman, habitually dressed in a blue tee shirt and jeans, with a white baseball cap jammed down over her curly black hair and a silver cross looped around her neck. Gloria had seen something of the world. Having lived for years in L.A., she spoke perfect English. She had met Alfred Von Bachmayr on one of his previous projects in Anapra. She even lived in a house roofed with one of his pallet creations. Gloria was Anapra's version of Mother Courage, coping with one rambunctious son. (The other son was more docile than his brother.) She drank beer but preferred tequila. "Two tequilas and I'll dance on that," she told us, gesturing to the long fold-up table where we ate our breakfast and supper.

One day we took some time off to help the women at Las Abejas fashion a sandwich board sign, which they installed in the median of the road that ran past the restaurant. As far as we knew, this was their only advertisement. My contribution: I learned how to say "hinges" in Spanish, walked down the street and bought them at a hardware store called Mas Barrata (Cheaper). Our sign got blown over a week later by a powerful dust storm that plowed through the barrio.

By the end of the first week, we had lifted all the trusses up to the roof. Dean Coil and I took some time off to do some laundry on-site. This meant immersing our dirty clothes in a five-gallon pail, sloshing them around in sudsy water, then hanging them on a clothes line strung between a skewed pole and the wall at the back of the yard. A pair of my jeans dried stiff as wood pallets, but at least they were cleaner than when they had gone into the pail.

We were ready to insulate the south and east elevations of the restaurant. First, the straw was doused in a mixture of mud, clay, and water, which we churned like butter in an enormous barrel. It had the consistency and look—but undoubtedly not the taste—of chocolate pudding. Getting a pail full of the mixture and hauling it to a concrete slab to pour over a batch of straw took serious strength. We threshed the mixture to coat the straw evenly. Then we carried pails of the goop across the yard to the restaurant where we crammed it between the studs. The straw/chocolate pudding was held in place by two slip forms screwed into the studs, one above the other. After a couple of levels of insulation had been packed in and left to dry, the bottom slip form was unscrewed and repositioned above the one still in place, in a kind of leapfrogging technique to retain the insulation as it rose, layer upon layer. Variations of this technique are found elsewhere in the world. It is generally known by its French designation, pisé. We rammed in each layer with two-by-four boards. In Spanish, the word for straw is *paja*. Our constant need for it led to what Gary Aitkins called a mantra: "*mas paja*." Evaristo was the most enthusiastic of the straw hawkers among us. He charged back and forth, pushing a wheelbarrow of the straw-chocolate goo between the threshing slab and the restaurant. As he ran, he bellowed out our mantra, "*Mas paja, mas paja!*"

A second mishap at the worksite, this time my fault: while taking down some of our scaffolding, I lost my grip. Part of the scaffolding came crashing down on a screen door, gashing a V-shaped hole in it. Gary Aitkin, ever resourceful, and a volunteer from Las Cruces sewed the hole shut with a strand of electrical wiring.

Our project was garnering a dollop of recognition in Juárez: one afternoon a group from across town came to have a look at our work. The group was called Bitechi. A sort of Grameen Bank–type operation, it loaned small sums of money to families too poor to finish their modest houses. The boss was a Salvadoran named Mauricio Castaneda. He was accompanied by a Mexican architect, Aylette Galvan. Despite being well advanced in her pregnancy, Galvan clambered up a ladder to inspect the trusses on the roof. A few days later, some of us returned the visit, driving across Juárez to the Bitechi office. As luck would have it, Alfred's Toyota merged with an army convoy. We were squeezed between two trucks in a column of army vehicles. The front truck had a machine gun bolted down on its cab. We did not know it at the time, but this was the opening phase of a war between Mexican drug cartels that would empty Ciudad Juárez of much of its population over the next two years. Five thousand people would be slaughtered, and this city of two million souls would be paralyzed. The army—Los Federales—had been called in the day of our arrival to restore order to the disintegrating city. They did not succeed.

Bitechi had expansion plans. Castaneda asked Alfred Von Bachmayr about using the shack in front of Casa Emaus as a kind of Bitechi branch office for the west side of Juárez. The organization had made a total of six thousand loans in eleven years. Funding for Bitechi came almost entirely from U.S. sources like the Ford Foundation, although one maquila—Johnson & Johnson—did participate in the program. As to the shack in front of Casa Emaus, Von advised Castaneda to raise the issue with Padre Pablo, since the property was owned by the Columban Order. Castaneda pointed out that converting the shack to a Bitechi office presented a design opportunity for World Hands Project.

I began to develop a thirst for something other than the water that we habitually drank at supper. There was a hole-in-the-wall grocery store just down the hill from Casa Emaus. I was sure that like all the other *abarrotes* in Anapra it sold beer. Dean Coil advised me to take precautions. Local hoodlums—called cholos in Mexico—had once waylaid him—remember that Dean is a strapping six-foot-plus Scandinavian type—and made off with his spare change. Take one route to the store and another one back, he advised me. The store was tiny but packed with boxes and cans of comestibles, fresh fruit like bananas and apricots, and a variety of Mexican beers. I made my choice—Tecate if I remember right—and made my way back home. Keeping in mind Dean's admonishment, I plowed uphill through ankle-deep dust, skirting the abandoned school bus in front of the house. No cholos barred my path. I repeated the operation the next day with equal success. In fact, I never had a run-in with any lowlife types during the two weeks that I lived in Anapra. But I rarely ventured out alone and never after sunset. We worked as a team, lived as a team, and pretty much partied as a team.

It was our first weekend since the beginning of the project. Dean Coil's fiancée came by bus up from Chihuahua to join us for a couple of days. Her given name was Lupita, but Dean's nickname for her was Tiger Lily. None of us knew the woman, and we felt that to call her Tiger Lily would be too forward. Her bus from Chihuahua arrived late in the night, so we decided to meet her in the center of Juárez where we had supper at a place called the Kentucky Club. This is a famous watering hole, a favorite of Ernest Hemingway when he came to town, a wood-paneled pub with wood beams running across the ceiling. Green glass lanterns hung in front of Palladian mirrors behind the bar. The Kentucky Club served cold beer and sizzling hot shrimp fajitas. Dean knew one of the bartenders, a man who had spent time in the States and spoke unaccented English. He had returned to Juárez to raise his kids. It was a matter of family values, he said. Two weeks after we talked to him, the police busted the man for transporting cocaine from Mexico to the U.S.

Tiger Lily arrived just as we were finishing up. She had taken a taxi from the bus station on the east side of Juárez to the center of town. She was a handsome woman, with mid-length black hair and black eyes, nearly as tall as Dean. Her English was functional, certainly better than my Spanish or Erin's. With Dean, she spoke only Spanish. We returned to Anapra the way we had come in, on a municipal bus. Bus schedules (and routes) were something of a mystery, at least to me. Juddering over the unpaved streets of Anapra, the bus—our #10 lacked both shock absorbers and muffler—offered something of a joy ride, something to knock your teeth loose, and at night there was only the sickly pale glow of ceiling lights to see by. The bus was crammed on weekends with young people: poker-faced boys, their skinny legs squeezed tight together, sitting beside girls in party dresses, chattering like magpies, off for a night of fun in a Juárez dance hall, some of it innocent, some less so. The sign in the window opposite me read: *Ni tire basura*—don't litter.

Breakfast on Sunday was more relaxed than usual since this was a non-workday, and we had Lupita as our guest. Conversation drifted from one subject to another before settling on one that was becoming a lodestone for me: Father Joe. Dean Coil knew the priest best. Von scarcely knew him at all and only through a previous encounter in Anapra. Who was this enigmatic man? Why had he been tossed out of Mexico? The only Catholic priest in the history of the country to be deported for working without a work permit. Would it be possible to meet him? He lived a few miles away, across the border in El Paso. Dean promised to do what he could.

Later that morning we strolled down to the main street of Anapra. This was the site of a Sunday market called *Segundo*. Everything from plastic toys to work shoes was for sale. The Segundo spilled over both sides of the street and down the median. We had come down for a splash of local color and to offer moral support to our colleague Evaristo, who had staked out some space on the median. There he had lined up plants from his nursery. When we got to him, Evaristo told us what had happened earlier that morning. He had arrived at 5:00 a.m. Shortly thereafter, a motorist had come to a stop just in front of Evaristo's space. A couple of cholos jumped out of nowhere. They rushed the car. One of them had a knife. He jammed the blade into the driver's body, first slicing his neck, then sticking it up to the hilt between the man's ribs. They pulled him from behind the steering wheel before making off with his car. Evaristo was shaken to the soles of his *zapatas*. Later he told us that the motorist had died.

That afternoon Dean Coil and I accompanied Lupita to the bus terminal where she caught a bus back to Chihuahua. Erin had missed mass earlier that day in Anapra, so we took her to the cathedral in downtown Juárez. Dean and I wandered around the starkly modern building that housed El Centro de Arte while Erin attended mass. Afterwards we killed more time by chatting to Dean's drug-trafficking buddy at the Kentucky Club. Then we went back to the cathedral to wait for Erin. Our blond pixie was ecstatic: she had understood enough of the sermon to know that it dealt with the appearance of Jesus on the road to Emmaus. This, she told us, was one of her favorite Bible stories. The name of the town was also that of our dwelling place in Anapra.

Early the next week—the day, in fact, when some of us had joined the Mexican army to visit the Bitechi office in east Juárez—there occurred the third and final accident of the project: Erin Campbell shot a staple from our staple/nail gun through two of José Bernal's fingers. Work came to a halt while we sought medical assistance. The local clinic was closed, but eventually Von Bachmayr located a hospital

where José got a tetanus shot. Then he had his fingers bandaged. They stayed bandaged for a couple of days. But José did
not lose a day of work.

The dust storm that toppled the sandwich board advertising Las Abeyas came in from the southwest, and it came
in strong, with a wind fierce enough to rip the exposed straw
insulation off the restaurant roof. The storm did damage, not
to our building but to our director. Von Bachmayr had had
a cornea transplant two weeks before our project in Anapra.
The day after the storm, he complained of discomfort in his
left eye. True enough, that eye was alarmingly bloodshot.
We insisted that he consult an ophthalmologist in El Paso.
Friday afternoon, Von returned from his appointment with
a patch over his left eye. The doctor had removed a particle
of dust from his eye.

The storm continued for twenty-four hours. We carried
on, hauling straw to the roof, sprinkling it with a mud and
water mixture jerked up to the roof in plastic pails. Face
boards were cut and holes caulked, all in the teeth of a desert
gale. Tons of dust particles filled the air, including the little
varmint that sabotaged Von's artificial eye lens. When vis-
ibility dropped to a few feet—the houses across the road
were blanketed in a yellowish-brown fog—we packed it in
for the day.

To raise our spirits, Gary Aitkin and Erin Campbell
improvised a way to make chocolate chip cookies. They
had neither chocolate chips nor brown sugar. Never mind.
Hershey bars, broken into little chunks, white sugar, even
M&M's—our cooks had bought out Anapra—were all avail-
able. Erin phoned home to get her grandmother's recipe.
Casa Emaus became, overnight, the cookie capital of north
Mexico.

Accidents notwithstanding, our fame continued to
spread, at least in Juárez. A newspaper crew came out to
interview us and to photograph our work. Their article

appeared in *El Diario* on the Saturday before our departure. Erin bought two copies to take back home. Our sponsors, Las Hormigas, came to the restaurant to compliment us on our work and to congratulate everyone on the article in *El Diario*.

But the clock was ticking on the project. It was clear that not everything would be finished by the time we strapped on our knapsacks and decamped. We had insulated the building, but the solar water heater that we made out of a salvaged cylinder encased in tin wrapping never left the ground. (Its final resting place was to be on the roof, where it eventually came to rest, but only after we had taken our leave.) Nor did we have the time to plaster the walls. We did manage to get our hands dirty concocting various sample mixtures of clay and sand. We smeared these on the south wall, like poultices on a straw skin, to see how they looked and how they would weather, each sample tagged with the proportions of clay to sand—1:1, 2:1, 1:4. The decision on what proportions to use and the plastering itself were left to a later workshop. None of us realized at the time how violent, how chaotic, Juárez would become over the next two years as drug cartels battled over turf. Be that as it may, the plastering was completed and the water heater hoisted into place before all hell broke loose in the province of Chihuahua.

Following Alfred Von Bachmayr's lead one night, I paid for a four-hand massage at Clinica Santo Nino. Two heavy-set, middle-aged women, Sophie and Lucy, took care of me. They played New Age music—I remember a CD of native flute and a gong—while they rubbed me down by the light of a feeble lamp. The massage didn't last long. One of the masseuses had an autistic child with her. The other woman had bronchitis.

Next door, the night ended with a viewing of a DVD called *Crossing the Border*. The video showed the trials faced by people trying to cross Mexico from Central America to the U.S. Some sympathetic Mexicans would toss food to the emigrants riding the tops of freight trains. There were obstacles long before the Central Americans arrived at the U.S.-Mexico border. Gangs preyed on these people, refugees, in effect, fleeing their homelands. The most notorious of these was an organization called Mara Salvatrucha, otherwise known as MS-13. Its roots go back to Salvadoran neighborhoods of east L.A., where it arose to protect its fellow countrymen against other gangs. But it soon morphed into a pack of vicious killers and extortionists. U.S. authorities deported some gang members to their homeland, but this only spread the contagion. From El Salvador, the gang crossed into neighboring countries like Honduras, where it committed horrendous crimes, e.g., murdering twenty-eight people, children included, on a public bus in Tegucigalpa in 2002. Dean Coil told me that he had seen members of MS-13 in Anapra. Each was recognizable by a mosaic of tattoos, writhing across his upper torso and face. These made a gang member look like a Maori warrior. During our stay, none appeared. Nor did the local cholos ever accost any of us, possibly because our work was respected by the residents of Anapra.

Our last full day of work, Dean Coil put together a barbeque lunch. José Bernal did the actual cooking. His fingers were no longer bandaged after their stapling by Erin. He used some of the sticks from the dismembered pallets for his fire. Then he put an iron wok on top. His stir-fry consisted of strips of beef and onion slices. It was the best meal we had in Anapra during our two weeks there. As memorable as it was, our barbeque was eclipsed by a Saturday night fiesta at Las Abeyas. The work may not have been 100 percent finished, but we celebrated anyway. Gary Aitkin brought out his banjo, Erin Campbell her guitar. They sang a ditty about the two-week project, roasting everyone who had taken part. There were emotional goodbyes, because early the next day,

Sunday, in part to beat the traffic, some of us boarded the Toyota truck, others an asthmatic jalopy loaned to us by Gloria. We drove back across the Stanton Street bridge to the U.S. My nagging paid off: Dean Coil managed to arrange a get-together with the man himself. Midmorning, Father Joe strode into an El Paso restaurant. He was tall and handsome. Man, how he could talk! It was hard to describe him physically without falling back on clichés. The need to delineate him in psychological terms and in a theological context will come in the course of time. Father Joe was dressed not in a clerical dog collar but in jeans and a windbreaker. He spent two hours talking about the events that had led to his expulsion from Mexico. I scribbled maniacally on table napkins that Gary Aitkin kept feeding me across the table. In a sense, that collection of coffee-stained tissue paper is the origin of this book.

There followed a second round of goodbyes. The Santa Fe contingent, with Gary Aitkin in tow, drove north up to Las Cruces and I-25. Somehow Dean Coil coaxed Gloria's automobile to the airport, where he let me and Erin off before turning back to Ciudad Juárez. I was standing in line at the check-in desk when I heard a familiar cry. *Mas paja! Mas paja!* I turned around to see her, a blonde ponytail swishing past in the crowd, Erin Campbell in pursuit of her own flight and the rest of her life.

SETTLING SAN JUDAS

"We are not saviors."

That is what the ex-nun Lina Sarlat told one journalist. "This is slow, underground work." She spoke of their crusade to help women in a country that has historically treated females as inferior beings. "It requires patience," she said. "That's why we call ourselves *Las Hormigas*."

After their arrival in San Judas, Sarlat and Villalobos, both in their forties, opened a counseling center. Other projects led to the women's collective restaurant, Las Abejas, which Alfred Von Bachmayr's team had insulated. The prospects for success were good since the restaurant stood on the main highway passing through San Judas.

Helping women was the focus of their work. It was a self-evident need. One contributing factor was a shift in the Mexican economy. Traditionally Mexican men worked for pay, while their wives stayed at home performing domestic chores. But low-wage factories sprang up everywhere along the Mexican-U.S. border in the 1990's, in the wake of the passage of NAFTA. Juárez was no exception. Called maquiladoras—or maquilas for short—these factories generally employed women. So it was the women who became the bread-winners of their families. Denied their traditional macho roles, unemployed husbands stayed home and drank tequila, took drugs, turned violent.

Men were killed during the last decade of the twentieth century, but it was the murder of women that caught the attention of the media. It even became the subject of 2666, Roberto Bolaño's celebrated Spanish-language novel.

Amnesty International did a study of what came to be known as the "femicides" of Juárez. It found that at least 137 of the female victims had been murdered by sexual predators. Many of them had physical similarities: they were slender and pretty and had dark skin and long hair. A criminology professor, Julia Monarrez, commented, "I don't know if they are drug gangs, crooked policemen, or powerful politicians, but there is definitely a pattern to some of these crimes." A Mexican weekly listed 727 disappearances between 2010 and 2014. Many more such crimes occurred from the early 1990s onward.

A cluster of pink crosses erected on a butte overlooking San Judas, the scene of several of the murders, bore witness to the women's deaths. Nine of them. Their bodies were discovered over a period of time. Residents carried out a grisly search to uncover the corpses, some in shallow graves, most just dumped in ditches. Of some, little remained but a skeleton. One young woman, who had worked in one of the maquiladoras nearby, was identified by the color of her blouse and the white rubber bands that held her pony tail in place.

Authorities never satisfactorily solved the murders, although they contended otherwise. More often than not, police did not even investigate the crimes. Two bus drivers were arrested in 2001 for serial murders. They were made-to-order scapegoats: Juárez bus drivers had a rotten reputation for their treatment of women. One victim of a sexual assault—one who actually survived—accused a bus driver of the crime. When the driver was apprehended, he implicated four other men. Three of them were bus drivers.

In August of 2013, a woman wearing a blond wig boarded a downtown bus and shot the driver point-blank. No one seemed to take much notice of the killing. Violence had become pervasive throughout the city. The following morning, however, the blond vigilante struck again, this time after boarding a bus in a different part of the city. Now Juárez perked up its collective ears. "It was floating in the air that these bus drivers had committed sexual aggression," commented the former head of the local forensics unit, Oscar Maynez, "and she was taking revenge."

Not all bus drivers, however, were guilty as charged. Two bus drivers arrested in 2001 confessed to the murder of eight women, all of whose bodies had been found in one small cotton field. The police bragged that their efforts had led to a successful conclusion "to this sad episode." But burn marks on the two men's legs and abdomens, clearly visible in newspaper photos, suggested that the confessions had been extracted by torture. One of the bus drivers told a reporter that the cops had crushed lighted cigarettes on his genitals. This was totally untrue, declared the deputy attorney general of Chihuahua: the men had burned themselves while smoking.

Years later, both drivers were exonerated of the murder of the eight women. In the meantime, even with the bus drivers in detention, the killings went on.

Domestic violence accounts for a sizeable chunk of the murders of women in Ciudad Juárez, as elsewhere in the country. As already noted, women had begun to work in the maquilas of Juárez, while their men folk stayed home, overturning the social structure of the Mexican household. But this does not account for the murders in San Judas or for their sadistic nature. Victims had been raped, their hair pulled out by the roots. They'd been butchered with kitchen knives, burned, stomped on, and sliced up. Why? If there was a motive for the systematic killing of women in the 1990s, it was never uncovered.

The long and the short of it is that Ciudad Juárez acquired an international reputation for misogyny. Other countries in Latin America also have bad reputations for the way women are savaged. But lest we forget, lest we become too self-righteous about the situation in our own country—the U.S. racks up on average four thousand killings of women every year.

A march through Juárez on the tenth anniversary of the first of the femicides in the city drew tens of thousands of feminists, including celebrities like Jane Fonda and Sally Field. The protesters marched down Juárez Avenue through the center of Ciudad Juárez to the international bridge that connects downtown Juárez with El Paso. Flanking Fonda and Field, demonstrators held a long red banner that read "until the violence ends" in Spanish and English.

"One of the horrors is feeling that you don't matter, that what happens to you and your family has no impact, there are no ripples, you just don't count," Fonda told the British newspaper, the *Guardian*. "Part of our coming here is to show these mothers that we are hearing and we do care."

The day of the march culminated in a performance of Eve Ensler's *The Vagina Monologues* before an audience of four thousand people. The playwright jumped onstage at the conclusion of the play to proclaim before the cheering crowd that Juárez was "the pilot project" for "vagina warriors and vagina-friendly men."

"We are about making sure Juárez becomes the new capital of nonviolence towards women around the world," she said.

"Let's think about Juárez as the victory place."

★

San Judas came into existence in the 1970s when a retired civil servant, Luis Molino, received permission from the federal government to start a farming commune on a site to the west of Ciudad Juárez. There was an understanding that the land was federally owned and that Molino would not need to purchase it from private owners. Each of the 170 families who accompanied Molino to settle the area was given two hectares—about five acres—to cultivate. Authorities thought the man was crazy since the area was virtually inaccessible, with no amenities like water and electricity. All it had to offer in those days was a spectacular view of the border country, a nighttime sky of silent stars, and a desert wind that whistled through the tinder-dry sagebrush. Molino laid out a settlement with a grid of unpaved streets. The names came from the federal government. Newcomers used their five acres to sow vegetables, plant fruit trees (if they were willing to risk failure), and pasture farm animals like chickens, pigs, and goats. They surrounded their properties with fencing salvaged from rusty box springs that they found scattered about the mesa.

Molino petitioned the Institute for Agrarian Reform for titles to the land. These never came. Nor did the Institute do a survey of San Judas to determine whether it was truly the property of the nation. This became the crux of the land dispute that developed three decades later, and which is the focus of this history. Official recognition of the settlers' right to be in San Judas came in 1975 when then President of Mexico, Luis Echeverria, declared San Judas national property. Title holders were invited to step forward to contest that decree if they chose. There were no takers. At least not for twenty-five years. According to the Mexican constitution, a settler who occupied land for five years had the right to buy that land if no other claim was made to it. The land belonged to those who tilled it. So said the Mexican revolutionary Emiliano Zapata. Obviously, that was how the *colonos* in San Judas felt.

They lived in a dicey neighborhood. Despite their attachment to the land, residents complained that they found themselves in "a nest of drug smugglers" who sped through San Judas in convoys of expensive cars with tinted windows. Coincidently or not, their apparent destination abutted a dumping ground for some of the women's bodies discovered in the 1980s. Late in the 1990s, settlers reported that there was a clandestine airfield to the west of the colonia. After that disclosure, sinister-looking men threatened their lives and shadowed them. The airstrip was later identified as one belonging to the local drug cartel. Mexican authorities ordered it to be destroyed.

In the years that followed Molino's settling of San Judas, Ciudad Juárez expanded in all directions. To the west, it encompassed Molino's agricultural commune, which was attracting more settlers.

As the barrio grew, the Mexican Federal Electric Commission added San Judas to its grid. Five years after Molino first appeared on the scene, a primary school was established. It boasted two classrooms separated by a corridor, and it bore the name of a Mexican educator, Alfredo Nava Sahagún. This was a volunteer effort a bit like the work at the restaurant that Alfred Von Bachmayr's group would insulate three decades later. The school project involved residents of the barrio working under professional supervision. They erected a cinder block structure with a galvanized steel roof. They trucked in materials from other neighborhoods of Ciudad Juárez. The government equipped the two classrooms with chalkboards and child-size tables and chairs. Work was completed in a surprisingly short time—two weeks, from start to finish. This showed the importance that the colonos placed on having such a facility for their children. Although he was barely old enough to begin school in San Judas, José Bernal attended a couple of years there before his family shipped him off to the States.

A small Catholic chapel also went up. It was a modest adobe structure with air vents high up in the front wall and one triangular window—a symbol of the holy trinity—above the door. The chapel was named after Jesus of Nazareth. This is where Father Joe celebrated mass on Sundays when he was assigned the parish in the late 1990s.

With amenities, San Judas drew settlers migrating from the south. Twenty years after Molino began his agricultural commune, two hundred families had relocated in the barrio. For the most part, their houses were shacks with tar paper roofs, but some—like Molino's—were substantial cinder block dwellings. Von Bachmayr's volunteers put up one of their pallet houses here in the 1990s. Colonos began to acquire what they believed would pass for proof of residence: utility bills and voter IDs. Not that these offered any proof of ownership, at least in the real world of the Mexican borderland.

A new if precarious life was taking shape for people, some of whom were fleeing the ravages of the North America Free Trade Agreement (NAFTA) that Mexico and the U.S., along with Canada, had signed.

These were farmers who, like the Bernal family, which had preceded them, emigrated from the south. The provisions of NAFTA drove these farmers into bankruptcy. Subsidized U.S. agricultural produce flooded the Mexican market. Local growers were powerless to compete against the U.S. corn and pork. They abandoned their farms, some to move north in the hope of finding employment in industry, others to slip across the border to take jobs for the agribusinesses that had ruined their livelihoods—adding an insult to an injury.

"After I killed a pig, I would butcher it to sell the meat," said one farmer from the province of Veracruz. But with the country flooded with cheap pork from the U.S., that was no longer profitable. "I did what I had to in order to survive, but I could never earn enough. Sometimes the price of a pig was enough to buy what we needed," he said. "Then it wasn't. Farm prices kept going down. When we couldn't afford to pay our electric bill, we would use candles. Everyone was hurting all the time."

The farmer's family had a small herd of cows so that they could give milk to neighbors who came asking for it. "There were people worse off than us." Eventually the family sold four of its cows and five acres of land to provide enough money to get the farmer and his wife to the north. They settled in San Judas, in fact, where they made do in a one-room shack. It was their intent to look for employment in the factories that were sprouting up all along the border. Not surprisingly it was the farmer's wife who got a job in a maquila one mile away from San Judas. The farmer stayed home and scraped by on the odd jobs that came along.

(Maquila, the shortened version of maquiladora, is actually a Spanish word in its own right. It refers to the portion taken by the miller who processes customers' grain.)

Some settlers had memories of their past lives that were more nostalgic than the NAFTA-induced heartache. One woman named Estella recalled how she had yearned for the juice and the nectar of the maguey plant. Maguey is the source of the agave syrup that appears in U.S. grocery stores. The plant grew abundantly near Estella's ancestral home in Zacatecas. *Agua miel* is what she called the juice that her *abuelo* (grandfather) used to give her for breakfast. She named the nectar *lagrimas* (tears) *del maguey*. It was candy-like and gooey. When drought struck the region, agua miel was just about the only thing to drink. Her grandfather told her that it was healthier than cow's milk. The juice had to be drunk the day the maguey was milked, because it fermented within twenty-four hours and became *pulque*. When her abuelo harvested the juice, he was careful not to damage the maguey, so that it would survive what he called its castration.

Maguey also grows in the north of Mexico, but there it is a runt of a plant, dwarfed by its sculptural cousins further south. So agua miel and pulque were relatively unknown in Ciudad Juárez until recently. When they became available, Estella persuaded her father to take her to a cantina in town so that she could drink some pulque. She expected it to taste like agua miel, since that's what it came from. Not quite. She spat out her first mouthful, telling her papa that the stuff tasted like pasteurized piss.

FATHER JOE

Historically Boston's North End is home to the city's Italian community. This is where Joseph Borelli was born. This is where he grew up. His family occupied a walk-up flat not so different from others in the North End. It was furnished with chairs with white cotton stuffing that bulged out at rips in the seams. Crocheted antimacassars covered their arms and backs. These doilies were as white as the cotton stuffing and they were starch-stiff. Glossy renderings of the Sacred Heart of Jesus and the Virgin Mary in peeling frames lined the walls of the bedrooms. An opaque view of the Grand Canal in Venice, like a daguerreotype, hung in the parlor. This was a room that was used only for weddings and funerals. Except for breakfast, which they consumed clustered in front of the fridge, the family ate at a table in the kitchen. On Sundays and special occasions like Christmas, Mrs. Borelli spread a flower print cloth on the linoleum surface of the table.

Until it closed in 1974, Joe's father worked in the navy yard in Charleston, across the harbor from Boston. His mother stayed home and did housewifely things, which included all the duties incumbent on raising three lusty boys. Joe was the oldest and the rowdiest.

Mrs. Borelli spoke English normally, but Italian proverbs—and she knew them all—lost their pungency for her when translated into Yankee speech.

Dal frutto si conosce l'albero.

That was one of her favorites. Why Joe's mother should reprimand Joe for doing anything that reminded her of her own or her husband's failings was something of a mystery. Joe Sr. had family roots in Sicily. He was a quiet man who divulged little of what he thought about social issues and politics. When he wasn't working, he spent time with his cronies, drinking abstemious amounts of *birra Moretti* in a tavern on Hanover Street. Or else he stayed home, reading the sports section in the *Traveler*. That was how Joe would remember his dad: with his shirtsleeves rolled up and his reading glasses sliding down his nose while he checked up on the Red Sox or the Celtics or the Patriots, depending on the season. Joe had his father's classic good looks. But he was not his father's son temperamentally. It was from his mother that he seemed to have inherited his assertive personality.

The family was devoutly Catholic and attended mass every Sunday at St. Leonard's, the oldest Catholic church in the North End. The Borellis did not have much money, but they saw to it that all of their boys went to St. John School, the school associated with St. Leonard's, which in keeping with the church itself was the oldest parochial school in the North End. It was located in North Square, at 9 Moon Street, cheek by jowl with Paul Revere's house. That house and Old

North Church were the leading tourist attractions of the North End.

St. John occupied a severe-looking brick building, where it had been established in the 1880s. When Joe Borelli started going to the school, it was staffed by the Sisters of St. Joseph. Besides the classes that they taught, the sisters also handled the catechism lessons that Joe and all his Catholic classmates were required to attend. Although Vatican II was in session while Joe was learning his catechism, the young Borelli got his instruction from the Baltimore catechism then in use. That meant memorizing the answers to deceptively simple questions.

Is original sin the only kind of sin?

Original sin is not the only kind of sin; there is another kind, called actual sin, which we ourselves commit.

What is actual sin?

Actual sin is any willful thought, desire, word, action, or omission forbidden by the law of God.

How many kinds of actual sin are there?

There are two kinds of actual sin: mortal sin and venial sin.

What is mortal sin?

Mortal sin is a grievous offense against the law of God.

Joe did what he was told to do. He memorized the answers to his instructors' satisfaction and made his first communion on schedule. His parents were pleased. They had expected no less. For Joe, first communion was just another segment in the patchwork of Italian life in the North End. It was linked inextricably to the smell of pizza and freshly baked bread; the All Saints Day parade when laymen carried banners through the throngs that lined the streets of the neighborhood; the loud and operatic Italian spoken by the old folks sitting on the sidewalk chatting with one another in warm weather. It was a seamless culture.

When it came time to leave St. John, the Borellis thought to send Joe to the Catholic High School in East Boston. Joe was not an outstanding student, but he was intelligent, and his sixth grade teacher, Sister Joseph of Arimathea, came up with a radical idea: Why not apply to the Boston Latin School? This was Boston's premiere public school, *primus inter pares*, commonly known by its initials BLS. It required an exam to get in. The Borellis had no idea what admission to BLS entailed, but they were willing to be guided by Sister Joseph of Arimathea. Joe applied, sat the entrance exam, and passed it. There was a whiff of "told you so" pride in the corridors of St. John. As far as the Sisters of St. Joseph were concerned, the Wops had shown the Yankee aristocracy what they could do.

Going to the BLS shook up Joe's insular universe. Left behind were the familiar rhythms of life in the North End. Portraits of distinguished alumni festooned the walls of the school auditorium of BLS. These included governors of the Commonwealth of Massachusetts and several signers of the Declaration of Independence.

Even after the election of John F. Kennedy to the presidency, BLS continued to be, in its teaching staff and administration, a bastion of Yankee protocol. No jeans. No tee shirts. No sneakers. A tie was mandatory. That did not bother Joe. St. John had had much the same set of rules. But there was still something strange about the rules at BLS, something that rubbed Joe the wrong way, made him feel as if he didn't belong, and goaded him to rebel against the system. But to avoid censure, it had to be a sneaky rebellion, nothing flamboyant, nothing he could easily be called on the carpet for. Hypocrisy was an art form for the young Borelli. But the foul-mouthed, "altar boy of a lad" was cautious about his transgressions. Doodling in his notebook (when he should have been doing math sums), pulling faces, and making furtive gestures; that sort of thing marked the limits of his resistance to authority.

Slacking off on his school work was another matter. What was the point of studying Latin and Greek? Six years of the former, four of the latter. BLS was saturated with classical language tags. Given its name, that should have come as no surprise.

Gallia est omnis divisa in partes tres.

Who the fuck cared whether Gaul was divided into three or thirty-three parts? Latin was a starch-stiff, dead language, pronounced differently from Church Latin. The Greek was classical Greek, just as dead as Latin and harder to learn. Grades were important here, and it was more difficult to get the high marks that he had accumulated effortlessly at St. John.

Semester followed semester at BLS, and Joe's situation did not improve. His grades were mediocre. His attitude toward the school was one of sclerotic hostility. Some classmates nicknamed him Signor Bore. After plodding through three years, and in clear danger of his third and final censure, Joe told his parents that he was calling it quits. He wanted a change in his life. A real change. Joe wanted to join the Navy. Joe Sr. had worked in the Boston navy yard, after all. Why shouldn't Joe follow in his footsteps but up a notch?

Not so fast, though. There was first the need to get a high school diploma. With BLS out of the picture, Joe studied for the GED (General Educational Development). After BLS, that was a breeze for the quick-witted young Italian American. Joe passed the GED exam, and in 1974 he enlisted in the U.S. Navy.

It was a liberating experience, at least in some ways. Like all recruits, Joe shipped off to Great Lakes, Illinois, for twelve weeks of boot camp. This was his first experience of life outside his native New England, and it was different. Joe became friends with a Hopi recruit from Arizona. He was a quiet, unassuming man with copper-colored skin and a hawk nose. His name was a Jaw Breaker: Secaquaptewa. At least that was how the Navy spelled it.

What some people would find regimentation, others would call discipline. Joe got the impression that he was being molded to fit a certain image of a man in the military. The idea was to develop team cohesion: if one recruit fucked up, the whole platoon suffered.

If he wanted to make the grade, then Joe would need to conform to a preordained stereotype: to make his bed a certain way; to do enough pushups to bust his gut; to polish his boots to a mirror-like gloss; to salute and stand at attention until the bones in his back ached; not to flinch when officers screamed obscenities inches from his face (spittle launched onto his cheeks and mouth); and at the end of the day, to get one lousy cap and his navy whites and call himself a sailor, with a certificate to nail to the wall. The Borellis, who attended the graduation ceremony, were proud of their fire-tested, alpha-posturing son.

Before Joe Borelli left Great Lakes, Navy assessors subjected him to a battery of psychological and aptitude tests. Thus it was decreed: Joe would train as an air traffic controller. To do that, Joe moved to a town in western Tennessee north of Memphis called Millington. Classes were held in a building appropriately called the schoolhouse. Each morning Joe and his mates marched to class. At the end of the day, they marched back to the barracks. Midday they marched to and from the chow hall, where they got an hour to chow down under the watchful eye of the chow boss. Joe decided that the Navy's motto might as well be: if in doubt, get the sailors marching.

The program at Millington consisted of three phases. The first of these was exclusively class work, designed for the students to obtain their Federal Aviation Authority license. The second phase of the AC program was called the control

tower phase. In Joe's day, this involved moving models of
aircraft attached to sticks across an airfield configuration
printed on a surface the size of a ping-pong table.

The third phase of air controller school was the radar
phase. Most sailors considered this the fun part of their
training. When they got to radar study, the end was in sight.
There was a light at the end of the academic tunnel. And
with light, there came a job assignment. For Joe, this meant
transferring to the Navy's principal air station at Pensacola,
Florida.

Joe Borelli's first impression of Pensacola was one of
bewilderment. There was all the equipment, thousands, yes,
millions of dollars' worth of equipment. Joe was scared shit-
less to touch anything, even to ask questions about what he
saw. Exposure to Navy hardware was a humbling experience. He shared a room with a fellow cadet, a diffident and
religiously disposed rube whose home was a four-hour drive
downstate. Their room was a good deal spiffier than what the
midshipmen had in their barracks.

The regimen and the routine of military life, were not
so different from BLS, an institution often compared by students to Parris Island. But the Pensacola NAS had degrees
of liberty that the Latin School lacked. There was enough
time on weekends to go downtown, which was a short bus
or taxi ride from the Naval Air Station. Joe lost no time to
explore an exciting world of wine, women, and song. Or at
least what Pensacola had to offer: rum and tequila rather
than wine; rock 'n roll bands and bluegrass instead of lieder.
And women.

Ah, yes, the women. After the deprivation of the Boston
Latin School, Joe was eager to make up for lost time. And
there were opportunities. Joe was a good-looking gob.
Picking up women in bars was easy enough, once you got
past the awkwardness of the first few attempts. Weekends
melded one into another in a succession of encounters with

Southern girls who could spot the Navy dress whites two blocks away. The women were more than willing to share a few shots of Bacardi rum with Joe before showing him around town, driving off to the beaches to skinny-dip in the tepid water of the Gulf of Mexico. One weekend after another went by like this. Nothing stood out in a blur of unmemorable pleasure.

Joe's life had changed in a religious way as well. He stopped going to mass. The ingrained Catholicism of his youth had mostly evaporated in the fumes of Bacardi rum and Patrón tequila. His day-to-day existence had become, in the language of the Church, a spiritual desert. Yes, he had his Navy buddies, and, yes, he joked and guffawed with them, and, yes, they went barhopping in the raunchier parts of town. But something was missing. Joe's soul had shriveled up like a dog's turd in the Florida sun. His roommate sensed this.

"Come to church with me this Sunday?" the religious Floridian asked Joe. Joe thought over the invitation before deciding to accept.

This was how Joe Borelli tasted a branch of Christianity that he had previously known to exist but had never experienced firsthand. One thing seemed to lead to another. Joe succumbed to peer pressure and soon found himself attending Wednesday evening Bible study. His circle of friends widened to include young members of the church. One of these new friends asked Joe if he played an instrument? No, said Joe, but as a teen he had fooled around with a trap set. Would he like to play drums in the church band? Joe shrugged. Would he give it a try? Sure, why not?

That was the beginning of Joe Borelli's brief but intense career as a Jesus Band drummer. He played in a small combo named after the sponsoring church, the Living Word of Jesus Band. They played mostly for church functions. The lead singer, an auburn-haired woman named Leila, became his girlfriend. Not exactly your typical Southern girl, her family roots went back to Honduras and Lebanon.

Leila knew of Joe's Catholic background. One day, acting on a whim, she asked him if he would take her to mass. The request puzzled Joe, but he agreed. The next Sunday, he and Leila attended mass at a small Catholic church close to the Pensacola Naval Air Station.

A young and energetic priest celebrated mass. The service and the way it was conducted brought back memories for Joe. He found himself wondering whether he too might do what this priest was doing. A few days later, he discovered, tucked away in a corner of the *Navy Times*, an ad for a Catholic order called the Holy Ghost Fathers. This order, more commonly known as the Spiritans, was a missionary group that operated in Third World countries like Mexico. The Holy Ghost Fathers evangelized among the poor, among people who had not received the Word of God. They dedicated their lives to serving the oppressed. For several days Joe mulled over a decision to contact the order. Eventually he did just that.

Leila encouraged him. Had she been sent by the Holy Ghost? They parted as friends.

Could Joe hack the rigorous training demanded of its members? A lapsed Catholic, with serious doubts about any commitment to a life of celibacy, he was hardly an ideal candidate for the priesthood. Just give it a try, he was advised by a friendly father confessor. It was the same advice he had received on volunteering to play drums in the Living Word of Jesus Band. Once again, he decided to give it the old school try. Sister Joseph of Arimathea would have been so proud of him.

So the wheel had come full circle. His hitch up, discharged from the Navy, Joe enrolled in Duquesne University, Pittsburgh, Pennsylvania, where he studied Latin and Greek. These were the very same courses he had despised at BLS.

Still, he sucked it up and labored to master the dead languages, along with philosophy and theology. Years and years of philosophy and theology. After surviving that ordeal, he entered what was then the Spiritan seminary in nearby Bethel Park.

What can one say? Man proposes, God disposes. Somehow the Holy Ghost pulled Joe through. Or was it the Fathers of the Holy Ghost? In any event, on May 25, 1995, the youthful Joe Borelli joined a procession of white-robed men, some in sneakers and baseball caps, shambling into a church where he was duly ordained as a Holy Ghost father. The Spiritan Superior General in Rome, acting in consort with the U.S. provincial (head) of the Spiritan Order and Joe himself, gave young Borelli his marching orders to a poor neighborhood to the west of Ciudad Juárez, Mexico. It was called San Judas. Henceforth Joseph Borelli would be known to the world and to his future parishioners as Father Joe.

FAMILY MATTERS

By the 1990s, he owned all the filling stations in the city. He controlled dairy production and distribution throughout north Mexico. All the trucks on the roads of Chihuahua were licensed through one of his companies. All the tequila produced in the province came from distilleries that he owned. One of his companies was the country's largest transporters of liquid propane gas. He sat on the corporate boards of municipal commissions and half a dozen large companies that operated on both sides of the border.

His name was Pablo Schmidt, and he was one of the wealthiest men in Mexico.

His great grandfather Konrad had emigrated to Mexico in the mid-nineteenth century, at a time of social unrest in Germany. His wife and young son came with him. They were Rhineland Catholics, and they integrated smoothly into the public life of the country, at least on the level of religion. On other levels, however, the Schmidts maintained a self-conscious distance between themselves and the indigenous population of Mexico. The family retained a strong sense of its German identity. Culturally the Schmidts behaved as if they had never left the Old Country.

A merchant by trade, Konrad opened a general dry goods store in Matamoros. The business flourished, and the family bought land outside town. Konrad hired a handful of itinerant *vaqueros* and took to ranching. He also built a substantial hacienda where his family lived like *hidalgos*. Shortly thereafter Konrad's son Gustav married Doña Maria Romo.

The Romo family was large and influential in the border area. It even boasted a saint whose statue stands at the rear of the San Antonio cathedral of San Fernando. St. Toribio Romo was martyred during the Cristero Rebellion of the 1920s when the government in power went on an anticlerical binge. It began to confiscate Church property and to line up Catholic priests before firing squads. After execution, their bodies were hoisted on to telephone poles where they swung in the wind as a warning to the opposition. Everyone who fought in that war kept memories for the rest of their lives, like scar tissue in their souls.

Toribio, a priest, was a reluctant martyr of the Cristero Rebellion. On the night of his death, he was asleep in his bed, when a soldier broke into his room. Toribio woke up, admitted that he was a priest but pleaded, "Please don't kill me." These were the saint's last words. The soldier shot him point-blank. Toribio staggered out of his room before a second shot brought him down into the arms of his sister who had followed him outside. Pope John Paul II canonized twenty-six of the martyred priests. Of these, St. Toribio became the best-known.

Toribio became the patron saint of undocumented immigrants, popularly known as *Santo Pollero*—literally a little chicken. A vision of the saint is said to appear to migrants en route north, particularly when the going gets tough. Some believe that he made the migrants invisible to border agents.

Gustav and his bride decided to strike out on their own. They moved upriver to Ciudad Juárez and opened a branch of Father Konrad's store in the center of town. Again fortune smiled on the family. Business prospered, and Gustav expanded across the Rio Grande into El Paso and southern New Mexico.

The younger Schmidts prospered on a personal level, as well, producing two sons and three daughters. The older of the boys, Emanuel, was Pablo's father. He was a quick-witted if sly child who became his father's partner at a turbulent time in Mexican history. His brother Abel was utterly unlike Emanuel. A throwback to a more romantic age, he wore his curly hair long and read the poetry of Heinrich Heine and Rainer Maria Rilke, both in the original German and in Spanish translation. As a young adult, he became estranged from his family. Gustav tried to keep track of his son's whereabouts and what he was doing, but this was almost entirely through rumor.

Many of the events of the Mexican Revolution that occurred at the beginning of the twentieth century took place in the border region between Mexico and the U.S. This is where some of the most prominent revolutionaries resided. Revolutionary newspapers opened and closed every month in the Segundo Barrio neighborhood of El Paso.

Foremost among the revolutionaries was a swashbuckling type called Pancho Villa. That was the pseudonym for a man whose real name was José Doroteo Arango Arambula. Born a year before his sometime ally and fellow revolutionary, Emiliano Zapata, he seized the land of big landowners and distributed it to Mexican peasants. One of Pancho Villa's legendary exploits was to take control of Ciudad Juárez during the Mexican Revolution. His band of eight men captured Juárez with two pounds of coffee, the same amount of sugar, and eight hundred rounds of ammunition.

Pancho Villa roamed the deserts of Chihuahua and the American Southwest, seemingly at will. Americans knew him as the man who raided a U.S. arsenal in Columbus, New Mexico, killing eighteen soldiers and civilians. One rumor to circulate in Juárez was that Abel Schmidt had been among the Mexicans killed at Columbus. Gustav was never able to confirm that, even though he went to great lengths to do so. He even sought out postcards in El Paso, postcards produced in the aftermath of the Columbus raid, made from photographs of U.S. troops grinning broadly at the camera and propping up the bodies of dead Mexicans. Would Abel's body be displayed this way, like a big game trophy? Gustav never found any evidence of that. (Postcards like this were as common and as popular in their day as those depicting the carnival-like atmosphere of lynchings in Southern states decades later.)

Pancho Villa bequeathed Mexico a store of bloody anecdotes and secured for himself a niche in the country's pantheon of national heroes. His death was as sensational as his life: Driving back from his bank in his 1919 Dodge Roadster, he was ambushed by a covey of seven assassins who tore his upper body apart with dum-dum bullets.

By contrast, the leader of the revolutionary forces in the southern state of Moralos, Emiliano Zapata, left a more lasting and positive mark on the country. Born in 1879, he gained notoriety by protesting the seizure of peasant-owned land by a wealthy farmer. For his pains, he was arrested, then pardoned and inducted into the Mexican army. He served for only six months. Upon his return to civilian life, he resumed the peasants' struggle against landowners who would not stop stealing people's land. Zapata tried to have land restored by peaceful means, sometimes using ancient title deeds to establish claims. Increasingly, when that failed, he and his followers forcefully seized disputed land and distributed it as he saw fit.

Emiliano Zapata was a handsome hombre, what in Latin America is called a mestizo, part Indian, part Spanish. Photos of the man showed his face overshadowed by an enormous sombrero of the kind mariachi band members wear. Above his mouth spread a bristling handlebar mustache. Black circles lay beneath his deep-set, unflinching eyes. He was the iconic Mexican revolutionary.

In one photograph, taken in Zapata's younger years, he wore a basketball jersey, revealing the tattoos that covered his arms and upper chest.

Tattoos play an important role in Mexican culture. They go as far back as the early thirteenth century when they appear in both Aztec and Mexica codices. Dogs, snakes, and jaguars figure prominently in pre-Columbian tattoos. These animals are spiritual guides. They convey symbolic power to the men across whose biceps and pectoral muscles the animals frolic.

In colonial Mexico, the Catholic Church took a jaundiced view of tattoos, which it considered relics of a pagan past. This, of course, was true. One inspired the frontispiece for this book: a grinning, sombrero-wearing skeleton, strumming on a guitar and festooned with red roses. This is a figure commonly associated with the Day of the Dead in Mexico. Although *el Dia de Muertos* is a Catholic feast day, subsumed in All Saints Day, the skeleton has its bony roots in Aztec culture.

Mexican prison tattoos can be read like a book, explaining who the wearer is, what he is doing time for, and where he has been. The tattoos offer some protection in jail, since they establish a gang identity for the person tattooed. Tattoos acquired in prison are the product of a needle dipped in ink and drilled into the skin. Tear drops are a common tattoo: a tear drop indicates that the wearer has killed someone, and the number of tear drops shows the wearer's number of victims. They are like notches on a gunfighter's belt.

Tattoos serve a useful purpose as well as an ornamental one: they intimidate enemies. Black and grey tattoos, which originated in the barrios of the U.S., spilled across the border into Mexico where gangs, including gangs with a non-Mexican origin but with Mexican connections (think MS-13), use tattoos as gang logos.

★

At the beginning of the Mexican Revolution, in the early days of the twentieth century, a victory by Zapata's men and a simultaneous win by Pancho Villa in the north persuaded the president of the country to surrender power and flee to Europe. A falling-out among the victors of the revolution sent Zapata packing for the hills. The revolution continued, this time with a different government in Mexico City. Zapata's men—known as Zapatistas—adopted the slogan, *Tierra y Libertad* (Land and Liberty). "The land belongs to those who till it," Zapata said. It was probably his most memorable quote. But there were others worth quoting: "Since time immemorial, ignorance and obscurantism have produced nothing more than masses of slaves primed for tyranny." Or this one, which has a peculiarly Mexican flavor: "If you want to be a bird, then fly. If you want to be a worm, then crawl. But don't bitch when they crush you underfoot."

Emiliano Zapata's primary concern was the distribution of land to the peasants of Mexico. To this end, he established a Rural Loan Bank. It was the country's first agricultural credit union. A U.S. envoy who visited Zapatista-controlled areas of Mexico in 1917 contrasted what he saw there—what he called "the true social revolution"—with the disorder prevalent in the rest of the country. His description of the situation appeared in a series of articles published in the U.S. When these articles were read to Zapata, he said, "Now I can die in peace. Finally, they have done us justice."

Zapata's death was not peaceful. As in the case of Pancho Villa, assassins snuffed him out. The national hero of Mexico was killed in an elaborately staged ambush in the spring of 1919.

★

Despite his own tumultuous childhood in Germany, Gustav was out of his depth in coping with the ups and downs of Mexican politics in the 1910s. Not so the young Emanuel, who navigated the shoals of revolution with a canny sense of timing and the ability to assess accurately an ever-changing situation. By 1920, thanks to Emanuel's adroit maneuvering, the Schmidts of Ciudad Juárez emerged from the war richer and more powerful than ever before. In the process of securing the family fortune, Emanuel developed a kind of ruthlessness that was alien to his father and grandfather. He began to buy property from people whose claim to the land they sold was dubious if not outright bogus. Some of Emanuel's business dealings skipped lightly over the boundaries of legality. Bookkeeping in the offices of the Schmidts became a sleazy proposition. "That's the way things are done here," Emanuel said when Gustav questioned some of his son's entries. By implication, Gustav was too "old country," too rigid, to compete successfully in the modern world.

The Schmidts had long since assimilated into the life of the country to which Konrad had emigrated, at least on the surface. But a vestige of ancestral linkage remained. Long dormant in his grandfather and father, it glowed like an oxygenated ember in the depths of Emanuel's soul. This was not a business calculation. It was pure sentiment, an attachment to a country, to a culture and a history, and to a people he had never known. "*Sie sind muy macho,*" he told Gustav of the Nazis running Germany in the late 1930s, expressing himself in a mixture of Spanish and German. This was how the family spoke among itself, acknowledging the power of *das Dritte Reich*.

Then Germany altered its policies toward Mexico. Its submarines foolishly sank two Mexican freighters, and Mexico joined the alliance against Hitler in 1942. All Emanuel could do was to shrug and tell anyone who would listen that the situation had changed. There was no question that his reputation had been damaged. But a couple of good business deals soon glossed over the embarrassment of having chosen the wrong ideology and the wrong side of the war.

Emanuel was so busy making money and wielding influence that he postponed marriage far longer than was customary in Mexico. When he did finally choose a wife, she came—naturally—from another of the families of the business elite in north Mexico. Doña Patricia Gasset y Ortega was much younger than Emanuel. She could trace her family back to the conquistadores who arrived in Mexico from Spain in the early sixteenth century. Like Emanuel, she had an agile mind. Her ancestral pride morphed into arrogance as she aged. Friends and acquaintances understood this to be a projection of her personality, of her determination to have her way in all things.

The Schmidts' son was content to stand in his father's shadow as he grew up. In this respect, he did not take after Emanuel. Pablo led a cloistered life, educated in Catholic schools and befriending only children of his own background, wealth, and social status. Emanuel wanted his son to aspire to a career as an international businessman. It would be necessary, of course, for him to learn English and to develop contacts in the English-speaking world. So Emanuel made a radical decision, to pack his heir off to a tony U.S. boarding school, then to the most prestigious U.S.

university he could gain admittance to. First Hotchkiss in Connecticut, then Stanford in California.

Adjusting to life in the U.S. in the aftermath of World War II took some doing. But young Schmidt was exempt from the most savage anti-Mexican racism, since he came from "a better class of Mexican." All that made him more acceptable to his classmates, who even gave him an affectionate nickname, the Beaner. When they hazed him about being Mexican, he just shook his head, mumbled something unintelligible, and looked amiable. It was not surprising that his classmates' views rubbed off on him. These views, similar to those he had imbibed from his parents, reinforced the teenage Pablo's conviction that, yes, obviously he was superior to the bulk of his countrymen with their swarthy skins and Nahuatl/Yucatec features. Return visits to Ciudad Juárez and contact with his parents did nothing to alter Pablo's opinion of himself. Quite the contrary: these visits just reinforced his growing feelings of racial superiority.

Emanuel was pleased at how his son had turned out after his exposure to life in the States. Shortly after Pablo's graduation from Stanford and return home, he made him effectively a partner in his business. This was just as well. Emanuel's health was failing. His heart was now skipping every fourth beat. "You need more rest," counseled his doctors. "More exercise. Fewer tacos, no more empanadas."

"I can rest while I'm exercising," Emanuel declared. He was who he was and could not, would not, change his ways. So Emanuel Schmidt died of the consistencies in his character. His heart skipped its last beat while he was speeding on a desert road. He totaled his new Chevy by wrapping it around a telephone pole. Doctors in both Ciudad Juárez and El Paso tried to revive him but to no avail. Since his son was still a young man, his wife Doña Patricia became a sort of regent for family affairs. Business was something she was good at, since her instincts were sound, and she was as heartless as her late husband. Pablo listened respectfully to her directives, followed her advice, and bided his time waiting for when he could act independently of her. That time never came during her lifetime. Doña Patricia was too strong-willed to relinquish total control of the Schmidt empire.

Toward the end of Emanuel's life, the family had begun to dabble in philanthropic enterprises. It was good for business, Emanuel argued, since it enhanced the family's prestige. He renovated at considerable expense an orphanage associated with a local church and renamed it after the family. Outstanding students at Ciudad Juárez schools received awards, also named after the Schmidts. The family funded art fairs and gave generously to the Museum of Fine Arts. Seminarians wishing to pursue their studies at European institutions were eligible for stipends, renewable on a yearly basis. The Schmidts, of course, were on good terms with whoever the bishop of Chihuahua happened to be at any given time.

And there were other enterprises. Early in 1998, U.S. Immigration authorities uncovered a large stash of cocaine under the body of a liquid propane gas truck owned by Schmidt Enterprises. This occurred as the truck was crossing the border between Mexico and the U.S. Both countries launched investigations, but neither came to any conclusions, thanks in part to letters of support for the family from the governor of Chihuahua and a prominent U.S. senator. Other investigations concerning tax evasion and drug smuggling similarly came to naught. Pablo Schmidt led a charmed life as far as his entanglements with the law went.

As the years passed, Pablo came into his own, emerging slowly, painstakingly from the cocoon his parents had woven around him. He took Emanuel's place on the various commissions and committees his father had been a member of. And it was Pablo who, with the patience of an agile spider, continued to weave the web of relationships and alliances, both legal and illegal, Mexican and American, that Emanuel had begun.

Tirelessly the young Schmidt consolidated what his father had built up in Juárez, but NAFTA fundamentally altered the logistics of business in the north of Mexico. Pablo was quick to realize how that agreement made previously worthless land now strategically valuable. He rummaged among Emanuel's records and found something that piqued his interest. Apparently Emanuel had an interest in a swath of land to the west of the city that was so desolate that even the rattlesnakes gave it a wide berth. There was nothing as formal as a transfer of title, little more than a couple of letters and a few suspicious-looking stamps, but Pablo read into these documents the basis of a claim to a valuable parcel of land. It was the Schmidt family's equivalent of the Louisiana Purchase. The property in question lay on the route of a major highway, part of a system of roads that circled the El Paso-Juárez metro region and formed a leg of the NAFTA highway linking the three countries of North America.

This land lay in the colonia of San Judas. And it was the Schmidt family that owned it. Or so Pablo argued. This contention would have tragic and entirely foreseeable consequences.

La Jornada, January 11, 2000.

GENTLEMEN'S AGREEMENT

The buses arrived at 5:00 p.m. sharp. You could set your watch by them. And you could hear them before you saw them, since none of them had functioning mufflers. They juddered down the road, generating clouds of dust as they bounced over the rocks. In a previous lifetime, these vehicles had served as school buses in the U.S. Now they conveyed female workers back and forth from their low-paid jobs in the maquiladoras to the cinder block and wood pallet houses that they shared with their families. The factories where so many of the women living in San Judas worked—some of them for six days a week, fourteen hours a day—were entirely foreign-owned, mostly American but Korean and Taiwanese as well.

Maquiladoras predated NAFTA. They had begun to pop up along the U.S.-Mexico border when the braceros program, which had allowed guest workers from Mexico to take jobs in the U.S. without penalty, had been discontinued in the 1960s. The idea was that these factories would operate in duty-free zones. Materials were imported from the U.S. Finished products were exported duty-free back across the border. After the implementation of NAFTA at the beginning of 1994, the number of maquilas quadrupled. These sweatshops had a lousy reputation. Working conditions were often shockingly bad, mostly because there was no practical way to set up unions to protect the workers.

Here are a couple of for instances: one female worker attempted to get her factory, which produced paints, to provide masks to protect her and her fellow workers from paint fumes. The Mexican government's response to this request was to try to arrest the woman on charges of "destabilizing the maquiladora industry." She sought refuge in the U.S. There she filed a complaint against her company and the Mexican government. Need one note that nothing came of it?

A Korean-owned firm in Tijuana paid rock-bottom wages, when it paid them at all. Electrical cables charged with 440 volts wriggled through standing pools of water on the factory floor. Working spaces were unventilated. Streams of chrome-colored piss fouled workers' restrooms. The company was violating Mexican labor law left, right, and center, and government inspectors routinely filed reports of company abuses. None of these complaints elicited any response. A worker unloaded on his "union" rep who told him, "If you were paying me, then I would help you. But you do not pay me. The one who pays me is the company."

So much for the maquilas. What about NAFTA?

The concept of a North America Free Trade Agreement began in the 1980s with Ronald Reagan, but nothing concrete was achieved until Bill Clinton became president in 1992. The incoming Democratic administration had to decide on its priorities: Would it push first for a national health program, as Hillary Clinton wanted, or a trade agreement with Canada and Mexico? This is what Robert Rubin and other of the president's advisors advocated. And this is what Bill Clinton ultimately agreed to. During the 1992 campaign, Clinton had said that he would not support NAFTA unless it came with protection for workers' rights and environmental standards. After the election, his trade representative Mickey Kantor negotiated what were called side agreements, which aimed to do what Clinton had promised. But these side agreements stood outside NAFTA and did not enjoy the status of that agreement. In fact, they did little more than urge member countries to enforce their own labor and environmental laws. Member countries could ignore them with impunity: Mexico's finance minister went so far as to assure the Mexican business community that the side agreements were meaningless.

Some political observers believed that Clinton played his hand on the NAFTA negotiations ineptly. The President of Mexico, Carlos Salinas de Gotari, had bet the family farm on securing a trade agreement with the U.S. He would have had to accept, however grudgingly, provisions to protect labor rights and environmental standards with real teeth to them. The Canadians would also have come along. Clinton's failure to push on these safeguards would come back to haunt him.

Of course, there was resistance to the agreement from trade unions. They feared that U.S. workers would lose their jobs to cheap Mexican labor. Resistance also came from environmentalists. They worried that outsourcing production to our neighbor to the south would allow industry to evade antipollution regulations. Clinton's assurances were meant to allay the fears of these constituents.

Noam Chomsky produced one of the most prescient analyses of the outcomes of the agreement in 1994, the year that NAFTA went into effect. "The purpose of NAFTA," he said, "was to create an even smaller sector of highly privileged people—investors, professionals, managerial classes."

"It will work fine for them," the social critic warned, "and the general public will suffer." His most damning criticism of the pact came later:

> The search for profit, when it's unconstrained and free from public control, will naturally try to repress people's lives as much as possible. The executives wouldn't be doing their jobs otherwise.

The flashiest opposition to the agreement came from a Texas businessman who ran for president in 1992 (and again in 1996) as the anti-NAFTA candidate. Ross Perot contributed one memorable phrase to the debate over NAFTA: a "giant sucking sound." This is what the flood of jobs pouring into Mexico would generate. But Perot offered the pro-NAFTA forces a perfect straw man. It was easy to portray him as a clown, clueless about international commerce. His ignorance would imperil the country's struggle to emerge from recession. Or so his political opponents claimed. Clinton was endowed with formidable political skills. He managed to make Perot rather than NAFTA the issue.

NAFTA won in the U.S. Congress because Clinton muscled it through. There was a flurry of horse trading. One member of Congress said that he had been offered so many bridges for his district that all he needed now was a river. A former head of American Express said of Clinton that he had "stood up against his two prime constituents, labor and environment, to drive it home over their dead bodies."

The least that could be said about the price Clinton paid for double-crossing his allies was that it contributed to the Democrats' loss of the House of Representatives in the 1994 election. That set the stage for Clinton's impeachment four years later.

What about the prospective trading partners of the U.S.? They didn't really count in the overall scheme of things. "We are two very thin slices of bread and the top and bottom of a huge sandwich." Those were the words of one Canadian diplomat.

When all was said and done, was it worth the struggle? Here is the résumé of a rather lopsided balance sheet: two-way trade between the U.S. and Mexico expanded over a six-year period, rising from $100 billion in 1994 to $248 billion in 2000, one year after Mexico replaced Japan as this country's second largest trading partner. Laredo and El Paso, Texas, found themselves among the busiest ports in the country.

NAFTA supporters claimed that the agreement had created six million jobs in the U.S. In early 2006, Robert Reich, Bill Clinton's Secretary of Labor, made the point that the state of Ohio had gained three hundred thousand manufacturing jobs over the first two years of NAFTA. But in 2006, the state's unemployment figures rose nearly 6 percent from the spring of that year to the fall. What happened? Replacing human workers with robots was part of the answer. A transfer of job abroad was another factor, although Reich was quick to point out that American jobs went to China, not Mexico.

There was, naturally, another thoroughly caustic view of the matter, one that inspired a cartoon published in 2000 in a Mexican daily, the one reproduced at the beginning of this chapter. It showed a ragged Mexican campesina confronted by a stylishly dressed and bearded entrepreneur. It involved a play on words: when the entrepreneur, his arms spread wide to the heavens, intones in English the phrase "Free Trade!" the peasant woman—a hawk-nosed hag with a weary-looking kid in her shawl and an empty plate in her hand—cackles back "Free Joles!" i.e. frijoles, kidney beans in Spanish, a staple of the Mexican diet; the first syllable in that word is pronounced like "free."

The consequences of the agreement were indeed dire for Mexico. While growth had increased in Latin America to nearly 2 percent since 2000, Mexico's remained stubbornly below 1 percent. The poverty rate in the region has fallen dramatically since 2000, dipping from 44 percent to 28 percent. Over the same period of time, Mexico's has stuck a tad above 52 percent.

NAFTA allowed the dumping of U.S.-produced corn on the Mexican market. In 2002, for example, a bushel of U.S. corn sold for $1.74. But it cost $2.66 to produce. Federal government subsidies made up the difference. Mexican corn growers could not hope to compete with the subsidized price of U.S. corn. The result was that Mexican farmers were forced to abandon their land in droves—1.3 million of them, by one conservative estimate, followed in the footsteps of José Bernal's family.

The ruin of small corn farmers was, of course, predictable. It offered an example of what has been called the "creative destruction" of working capitalism: the inefficient wither away in the face of the more efficient. This is what the Salinas government and its successors wanted. The elimination of small Mexican farms provided a source of still more cheap labor for foreign investors in Mexico. Ten years after NAFTA came into effect, the *New York Times* asserted that "Mexican officials say openly that they long ago concluded that small agriculture was inefficient, and that the solution for farmers was to find other work."

But that was not so simple. In the ten years after its implementation, Mexico gained more than half a million jobs in the poor-paying maquiladoras that pimple the U.S.-Mexico border. But it lost one hundred thousand jobs in the non-maquila sector of its economy. The net result was to replace higher-paying jobs with jobs that paid less.

What's more, not all the displaced peasant farmers in Mexico could be absorbed by Mexican industry. One million peasants driven off their land were left unaccounted for. These bankrupted campesinos needed to earn a living somehow. So what became of them? A partial answer to the question is that some became itinerant farmers working for larger farms in Mexico. The complement to that answer is that they crossed the border as wetbacks and wanderers in the wilderness, some to work for the same companies that had put them out of business in Mexico. What had been touted as a benefit of NAFTA—that it would ease the illegal emigration of Mexicans into the U.S.—produced the exact opposite result. "If Washington wants to reduce Mexico's immigration to the United States," the *New York Times* wrote on March 3, 2003, "ending subsidies for agribusiness would be far more effective than beefing up the border patrol."

Illegal immigration into this country was a case of chickens coming home to roost. In an Orwellian twist, the failure of NAFTA to solve the problem of illegal immigration was seen as a potential success of the agreement. Some political commentators viewed the flood of Mexican workers who swarmed into the U.S. as a *solution* (of sorts) to the vexing labor problems in Mexico. It just needed a little tinkering to set things right. Unemployment and sub-subsistence wages drove Mexicans to swim the Rio Grande and to trek across the Arizona desert. What to do? Obviously, legalize what had been illegal: make the migrants legal residents of the U.S. Make it possible for them to stay on in the country as long as they were needed. That was just the ticket. "Free trade will not substantially moderate pressures for migration as long as the social and economic fundamentals continue to encourage movement," said Mack McLarty of the Clinton administration, one of the most fervent supporters of NAFTA.

It was not only American politicians who saw migrant labor in a positive light. One of Salinas' successors as President of Mexico, Vicente Fox, hailed the newly minted braceros of NAFTA as national heroes for sending back home billions of dollars of their pay.

There is yet another answer to the question about the fate of displaced peasants, and it is the most sobering. Many campesinos forced to abandon their fields found work in the country's drug cartels.

For poor Mexicans, NAFTA was a lethal proposition. In 1994, when the agreement came into effect, their minimum wage bought almost 45 pounds of tortillas. A little less than a decade later, it bought less than 20. The 24.5 liters of gas (for cooking and heating) that it bought in 1994 had—by 2003—dwindled to 7.

The border region between the U.S. and Mexico became a sliver of a boomtown. It could not cope with the influx of refugees from elsewhere in Mexico. It could not cope with the industrial pollution that the burgeoning maquilas produced. Toxic waste was dumped hither and yon, in the rivers and on the land.

★

One positive, if unintended, consequence of NAFTA's adoption was the meteoric growth of a homegrown revolt against the Mexican government. This one made headlines throughout the world. It was the Zapatista rebellion, which erupted on January 1, 1994, the day that NAFTA was launched.

As many as five hundred people, the overwhelming majority of them civilians, were killed in the first twelve days of fighting during the first month of the Zapatista insurrection. Shortly thereafter, one hundred thousand protesters filled the Zocaló of Mexico City to demand the withdrawal of the Mexican army from the jungles of Chiapas. Twenty years after it began, the revolt still controlled a handful of municipalities in Chiapas.

Who *were* these revolutionaries and what did they want?

The movement was named after Emiliano Zapata, the national folk hero who fought during the Mexican Revolution, which began in 1910 and continued sporadically for the next ten years. The Zapatista movement took shape during the 1980s in response to peasants' frustration with their situation in the country. The indigenous people of Mexico endured conditions tantamount to slavery. Preparations for NAFTA were the straw that broke the camel's back. At the insistence of the U.S., Carlos Salinas modified part of the Mexican Constitution—Article 27—which had provided the legal framework for the distribution of communally owned land called *ejidos*. By the time NAFTA came on the scene, about half the farmland in the country was in the form of ejidos. When Salinas acted to abolish them, there were literally thousands of ejido petitions pending before the Agrarian Reform Commission. With his obliteration of land reform, communities throughout the country lost all hope of achieving ejido status. Peasants were fed up with their government's neglect.

Zapatista groups in Chiapas began to consider whether they should unleash armed resistance to the government. Despite resistance from the Catholic Church, the decision was made to launch attacks on government targets. They pounced on the first day of the year 1994. While the ruling party was hosting a glittering gala at the Palace of Fine Arts in Mexico City, the Zapatistas—otherwise known as Ejército Zapatista de Liberación Nacional (EZLN)—were hacking their way through the jungles of Chiapas. They quickly seized the capital of the state, San Cristóbal de las Casas. Immediately thereafter, the insurgents ransacked the city's Palacio Municipal. They tossed the building furniture and the half-shredded documents that they had grabbed from the civil registrar's office into the square below. Then they doused the pile with kerosene and struck a match to it.

Eyewitness reports of what happened that New Year's Day conveyed the excitement that gripped the city when the Zapatistas took control of San Cristóbal and other localities in Chiapas. One observer—a journalist named Gaspar Morquecho—was returning to town after attending a party when he encountered a roadblock. He circumvented it by detouring through the parking lot of a filling station. When he arrived in the center of San Cristóbal, he asked one of the Zapatista soldiers what the hell was coming off. The man tore a poster off a wall where it had just been affixed and handed it to the journalist. Morquecho could smell the fresh glue on the poster. It was the movement's declaration of war against the government of Mexico.

Morquecho could not sleep that night. He roamed the city center at will despite the presence of Zapatista soldiers in the street. He was euphoric. After the failure of so many movements in the past fifteen years, he felt hope springing up in his heart.

"At last," he said, "something was happening in this fucking country."

The following day the army arrived in San Cristóbal. The Zapatistas melted back into the jungle. In fact, the EZLN had no realistic hope of defeating the government of Mexico and its army. Their mission, even in their own eyes, appeared suicidal. But the revolutionaries believed that their word was stronger than the sword or the bayonet or the MK-47 or anything else in their foe's arsenal. Theirs was what has been called a war of magic. The spirit, they believed, could vanquish steel bullets.

The bishop of San Cristóbal, Samuel Ruiz, brokered a ceasefire that ended the fighting later in January 1994. Although he had not condoned the Zapatista uprising, Bishop Ruiz was a well-known advocate of liberation theology—a movement in the Catholic Church that identified with the poor—and he was sympathetic to the plight of the indigenous people of Mexico. He was the right man at the right place at the right time. He lived with his flock, learning their languages, eating the beans and tortillas that they ate, and discovering for himself what their living conditions were like. He experienced a sort of conversion in reverse, and this set him at odds with the mestizo establishment of Chiapas, who called him "*el Obispo Rojo*" (the Red Bishop).

The bishop's offences included organizing peasant cooperatives and teaching Indian culture and traditions. "They are God's people, every one of them just as much as a white person is," he said of the indigenous people of Chiapas and, by extension, of Mexico and Latin America in general. "But one thousand Indians do not matter when one white person speaks out."

The Zapatistas' stress on autonomy led to the creation of governing groups, *juntas de buen gobierno*, whose members were selected to serve for one year. These groups, which governed regions under Zapatista control, gained a reputation for honesty and transparency. Given the movement's allegiance to autonomous governance, it was not surprising that no orthodox leadership emerged in the EZLN. Its iconic spokesman was known for the better part of his public life as Subcomandante (Sup) Marcos.

Marcos was not himself an indigenous Indian although it was hard to say what he looked like. He was always photographed wearing a black ski mask, sometimes with a skull-and-bones eye patch over the right eye. He was often seen smoking a long-stemmed pipe. The ski mask became the trademark of the Zapatista movement. It struck terror in the hearts of the ruling class. The government claimed that Marcos's real name was Rafael Sebastián Guillén Vicente and that he was the son of Spanish immigrants and had attended the Sorbonne in Paris, but there is no record of this.

Marcos is the embodiment of mystery. Like Jesus, he often spoke in riddles. He once said, when asked his age, that he was 518. He described himself this way:

> Marcos is gay in San Francisco, black in South Africa, an Asian in Europe, a Chicano in San Ysidro, an anarchist in Spain, a Palestinian in Israel, a Mayan Indian in the streets of San Cristóbal, a Jew in Germany, a Gypsy in Poland, a Mohawk in Québec, a pacifist in Bosnia, a single woman on the Metro at 10:00 p.m., a peasant without land, a gang member in the slums, an unemployed worker, an unhappy student, and, of course, a Zapatista in the mountains.

Marcos himself disappeared for four or five years at the beginning of the new century, only to reappear in August 2005, emerging from the jungle to preside over a series of meetings. Their purpose was to chart the next phase of the Zapatistas' struggle, la Otra Campaña, in order to avert a situation where "they will finish off the country before we are done."

La Otra Campaña would be peaceful. It would be a different approach to politics. The EZLN would respect "the privilege of the ear."

The revolutionaries launched their campaign on January 1, 2006, the twelfth anniversary of the Zapatistas' first attacks in Chiapas. Sup Marcos, still the most recognizable and charismatic of the movement's leaders, traveled the length and breadth of the land, touching down in each of Mexico's thirty-one states. He made the trip on a motorbike à la Che Guevara, and throngs of admirers, "chanting and whistling," greeted him. His ski-masked face appeared everywhere, on tee shirts, posters, and badges.

His message was simple and clear: Land to the Peasants.

And the Zapatistas were heard the length and breadth of Mexico. One man to hear their message and to take it to heart was José Bernal, Ojos del Lobo, the dark-skinned Mexican American volunteer who had grown up in San Judas and East L.A., the man who had worked on Alfred Von Bachmayr's insulation project in San Judas.

OJOS DEL LOBO

The extended Bernal family had always been a restless bunch. Two of José Bernal's uncles, both older than his Dad, had decamped for the U.S. years before, leaving only José's immediate family behind in the cornfields of Chiapas. But unlike his brothers, who had left voluntarily in search of a better life, José's father had no choice but to pull up stakes and migrate northward in the late 1970s. He did not wait for the advent of NAFTA to go bankrupt. He simply could not earn a living, not even on the rock-bottom terms of subsistence farming.

The family had no clear idea where they were going. Possibly the U.S. border. But they had no visas to enter the country. And they had very little money. So the Bernals made their way north to an uncertain destination with nothing in pocket to get there. Occasionally they took buses. Sometimes a kindly truck driver offered them a lift. One particularly harrowing segment of the trek placed them on the top of a freight train along with a bevy of other destitute voyagers. For the most part, these were Salvadorans, peasants fleeing the civil war in that country, but there was a mix of peoples from all over Central America as well as Mexico. Young José was thrilled by this train ride. He might have been terrified, but the train wasn't going fast and there was his reliable Dad to hang on to. People on overpasses would sometimes throw tortilla wraps to the migrants as they passed beneath them.

When the money threatened to run out, the family stopped, and José's Dad would find work as an itinerant laborer on a big hacienda. Along with other migrant workers, the family lived in a cardboard and wood pellet shack, separated by an eroded ravine from the owners' big house. Papa Bernal endured the contempt and physical abuse of the hacienda manager to earn a handful of pesos for picking corn, herding sheep, and slaughtering chickens. José saw how his father was treated. He shared his father's humiliation at the hands of managers who wore cowboy boots and vaquero hats and yelled orders at the campesinos under their command. But he was too young to articulate his feelings of injustice. That was just the way it was, perhaps the way it had always been. But it was still wrong, and young José determined quietly, in a childish way, that when the time came he would do something to put right what was unjust.

After a couple of weeks of tenant farming, the family continued to wend its way northward to an unpromising future, an unknown land, possibly the U.S.—but who knew?—a country where José had two uncles, a country that the Bernal family had no way of entering, no prospective status as legal immigrants, no papers of any sort. In a word, nothing.

The Bernals got to the border at San Judas. This happened not by design but by random happenstance. There they stopped. Papa Bernal was worn out. He didn't have the energy to scale fences or ford concrete-walled water conduits. The land without promise lay beyond his reach.

José's mother found work in one of the maquilas. His Dad cobbled together a shack of cinderblocks and waste lumber. It wasn't much, but it provided a shelter. It offered a degree of stability and routine in the life of a family that had known little of either for months.

For a couple of years, José attended the local school in San Judas, the one named after Alfredo Nava Sahagún. This was the two-room facility that the neighbors had constructed themselves. A nativity scene was pinned to the bulletin board at Christmas time. The Virgin Mary and Joseph, represented as starched and spotless Mexican peasants, watched with unassertive pride over the Baby Jesus. The divine infant was depicted with shining doll eyes, like a Pokémon figure.

José's textbooks came from Mexico City. There were five of them: math, science, Spanish, ethics and philosophy, and civics. José did math and Spanish every day. The other subjects were taught twice a week. In math, he liked figuring out the areas of geometric figures: triangles, parallelograms, and trapezoids. He was good at this sort of thing, and he did his sums quickly. Spanish was okay, but it was science that fascinated him. At an early age, he learned about human anatomy from full-color representations of the heart, the circulatory system, and the brain. His science book contained drawings of animals and plants native to Chihuahua. He pored over these for hours.

There were two teachers at the school in José's day: Señor Martinez, a sad-eyed disciplinarian who wore a baggy beige suit, a striped shirt, and an incongruously loud tie; and Señora Gomez, a youngish free spirit who affected granny glasses and encouraged her students to dream about their future. Neither teacher lived in San Judas. They both took the bus in from Ciudad Juárez. They taught anywhere from ten to thirty students squeezed into their classrooms. Each teacher did all the subjects in the curriculum. There was a map of Chihuahua in each of the classrooms along with a picture of Emiliano Zapata with his bushy mustache. Señora Gomez had tacked up a portrait of Che Guevara alongside Zapata.

Shortly after the move to San Judas, Papa Bernal's health began to fail. Possibly it was fatigue, possibly the lack of prospects for a better future. Possibly it was what an American psychiatrist would diagnose as depression. The classic pattern of working mother/stay-at-home dad weighed heavily on José's father. He developed a stubborn cough, which some days kept him in bed. He began to drink a lot of mescal, sometimes downing a bottle a day. At least he kept his sense of humor. He would look at his young son, at the dark honey color of his skin and call him an Aztec campesino. There was some truth in the joke, but the Bernals had Catalan as well as Indian blood in their veins. José developed strongly angular features as he grew, and there was the issue of his eyes, the subject and inspiration of his eventual nickname, a pale non-color that had the effect of startling, even amusing, people when they first encountered him.

Whether it was a premonition of things to come or a carefully thought-out precaution incubated by the misfortunes of his own life, who could say? But José's Dad wrote to his two older brothers in the U.S. Years had passed since they had left Chiapas. It was difficult to find a mailing address for the men, but the Bernals of San Judas managed with the help of neighbors and a local priest. They needed all the help that they could get, since the Bernals wrote and read so little Spanish they were functionally illiterate. Would they be willing to sponsor José if the family could complete the paperwork to secure the boy a visa? Both men, the boy's uncles, agreed.

When the paperwork came to a successful conclusion, the family scraped together enough money to buy José a bus ticket from El Paso to Las Cruces, New Mexico, where his younger uncle lived. It was the first José had heard about it.

"Why do I have to leave?" José asked his father tearfully as the family assembled the boy's meager belongings in a battered suitcase.

Papa Bernal ran his hand through his son's thick black hair. He said softly, "Things are better up there. You will have more of a future up there."

José remained quiet. He stared at his scuffed shoes with holes in their soles.

"You can come back when you want, too," his father coaxed him. "You'll be with family. Stay with your uncle and learn English."

José's stay with his New Mexico uncle was not a happy one. His uncle had his own family, which included two boys who treated José like the vaqueros had treated his father. His cousins called him the little Spic and made fun of his tattered clothes. The rest of the family talked half the time in English, ate cheeseburgers instead of enchiladas, and seemed hell-bent on assimilating into Anglo culture. The family's disdain for anything and everything Mexican confused and hurt José. Who were these freaks of nature whom his father had called family?

Six months after José came to live with his Las Cruces brethren, word came that his father had died. The cause of death, it was reported, was tuberculosis. José returned to San Judas for his father's funeral. He was buried in a patch of desert surrounded by a coyote fence and sprinkled with a handful of rusting crosses.

"I'll stay here with you from now on," José told his mother.

"No, you won't!" said his mother. "You need to go back. Otherwise you'll end up like your father. I have friends here now. I can manage on my own."

José shook his head. "I'm not going back to Las Cruces. I hate that place."

His mother frowned. She thought over what he had said. "You have another uncle in Los Angeles. That would be a better situation for you."

It took more paperwork, more trips to the U.S. consulate, but with help from the same set of neighbors and the same priest in Ciudad Juárez, Señora Bernal packed José off to his uncle in L.A.

Tio Antonio was older than his brothers. He was a taciturn, introspective man who rarely showed what he was feeling. He had served in the Korean War and had a Purple Heart and a Medal of Honor to show for it. These were kept in a wooden box on the buffet in the dining room. "I got shot," was all he would say when José asked him about the Purple Heart. About the Medal of Honor, he would say nothing at all. His own children, José's California cousins, had left their father's house to strike out on their own.

Tio Antonio and his wife Imelda lived in a Mexican American neighborhood of East Los Angeles called Boyle Heights. Their house on Soto Street was a bungalow, similar to other houses on their block. It had a pillared porch and iron grills on the windows. When the wind blew the right way, you could smell the hot bread in La Favorita Bakery on 4th Street. By comparison with what José had known in San Judas, it might have been the Palace of Versailles, but in Los Angeles it was a drab working-class dwelling in need of a paint job.

One day, walking home from school along Fickett Street, José passed a wall mural. He had seen it before but had not paid much attention to it. The mural portrayed the death of a young man dressed in a white tee shirt and brown pants. He lay in the arms of two friends, a man and a woman, while a brown-faced Blessed Virgin hovered overhead. Her arms were outstretched, all encompassing, as if waiting to receive the youthful victim into the blissful realm of Paradise. He was a gang member, José guessed, probably a member of Varrio Nuevo Estrada, the principal gang of Boyle Heights.

A couple of days later, when he was passing the same mural, José was stopped by two kids his own age. They looked a bit like his Las Cruces cousins, but their manner was more cordial. It had none of the hostility José had encountered on his first foray north of the border. "Hi," one of them said, "how you doing?" This and the rest of the conversation that ensued was in Spanish. José was guarded in his responses. "Would you like to come with us and meet some of our friends?" they asked. José was tempted. He wanted to fit in, to find friends, but his uncle had warned him to give the gangs a wide berth. Maybe, he told them, but now he had to get home. His uncle and aunt would be waiting for him. His new friends smiled and nodded and said that maybe another time they could all go off together to meet some of *los hermanos*.

Varrio Nuevo Estrada—generally known by its initials VNE—had begun as a sort of vigilante group to protect the Mexicans of the neighborhood. The white cops of L.A. didn't give a shit for the *peónes* of Boyle Heights. Someone had to protect them. Over time, however, VNE evolved into a criminal gang, one of the most notorious in the city. They branched out as well, spreading in the 1980s into other neighborhoods of central Los Angeles and some of the city's suburbs. Their raids on the other side of downtown L.A., in the Pico-Union district, led to the formation of a new vigilante group to protect the Salvadorans who populated the area. That was Mara Salvatrucha—the infamous MS-13— which followed the same descent into criminal conduct as VNE. MS-13 turned into what was possibly the most vicious of the Hispanic gangs to spring up in the Los Angeles area. With alarming speed, it became an international network of small-time punks.

Tio Antonio heard of his nephew's encounter with the local VNE. The old man had evaded the gang's grasp as a youth, but he knew his neighborhood; he had contacts everywhere, and he put the word out on the street that los hermanos were to stay away from his nephew. The VNE never again approached José.

José liked his Tio Antonio, even if his uncle had little to say to him. He enjoyed the grandfatherly man's company. He admired his courage and undemonstrative behavior. And he wanted to share more fully in his life. For years, Antonio had played guitar with a mariachi band that performed in Boyle Heights, mostly for weddings and baptisms. José knew this and wanted to take advantage of his uncle's musical connections.

"I want to learn to play the guitar," José announced one night after supper.

Tio Antonio had been dragging on an after-dinner cigarette. He looked noncommittal, neither for nor against the idea. "I can teach you the basics," he said finally.

And so he did. He brought out his guitar, placed the fingers of José's left hand on the frets and guided the fingers of his right hand over the strings. It was like witchcraft. José was mesmerized to hear the music that he made just by strumming. Soon José had the three chords for a simple melody.

"Practice," Tio Antonio advised him.

And so he did. He learned chord progressions, rhythms, then more songs. For his birthday, his Tia Imelda and Tio Antonio gave him a guitar of his own, a beautiful Spanish guitar. Where had they got the money? José did not ask.

One day, like a bolt out of the blue, Tio Antonio asked his nephew, "Would you like to join the band?"

José gulped and answered without giving the question a second thought: "I'd like that."

José could not believe the invitation that his uncle was extending. Would the band accept him?

Tio Antonio shrugged. "There's no harm in asking," he said.

Antonio's attendance at rehearsals had fallen off recently, and this caused problems for the band—called Los Lobos—but Tio Antonio's prestige in the neighborhood was such that his sporadic absences were accepted without censure. When he played, he did so like a guest performer.

Los Lobos wanted to hear the young man play. Fair enough. Tio Antonio taught José a couple of common mariachi songs, which he practiced until he had them memorized. One evening, during what amounted to an audition, he sang one of them for the band, accompanying himself on his new Spanish guitar. It was the well-known *Canción del mariachi*:

> I'm a very honorable man
> And I like the best things
> I don't lack women
> Nor money, nor love
> (*Soy un hombre muy honrado*
> *Que me gusta lo mejor*
> *Las mujeres no me faltan*
> *Ni al dinero, ni el amor*)

Los Lobos were pleased with their new recruit. "You did good, muchacho," the lead violinist praised him. The other band members nodded their assent. "You're one of us now," declared the harpist.

"He even looks like a wolf," the group's drummer joked. "Look at his eyes, the eyes of a wolf." Everyone laughed. The nickname stuck. José became the mascot for the band, Los Ojos del Lobo. Tia Imelda went to work and concocted a charro suit for him, not one with as much embroidery as what could be purchased in a store but something that would fit in with the rest of the band.

José's first gig was at a private party, the coming-of-age celebration for a fifteen-year-old girl, known as a *quinceañera*. The event took place in a church hall decorated with white and pink balloons and strings of confetti. The girl who was being feted wore an evening dress bristling with pink frills. She looked like a Walt Disney porcupine. Friends had had to shove her into the stretch limo that ferried her from her parents' house to the church. Her female attendants wore long pink dresses, and the males in attendance were dressed in stiff white shirts with pink bow ties. Their hair was gelled. They looked like clones of Rudolph Valentino in his role as the Sheikh of Araby. A cake half the size of the hall and covered in an inch of pink and white frosting occupied the center of a long trestle table.

Los Lobos played. The audience clapped and cheered. José felt comfortable. He knew that he was playing decently and that people were smiling appreciatively at him. He was Tio Antonio's nephew, after all, and the neighborhood was rooting for him. His uncle had come out of semi-retirement, brushing the lint off his charro suit, to play alongside of José. That bolstered young Bernal's self-confidence.

Waiting in line for a slice of cake, José caught the eye of one of the attendants in a pink dress. He smiled at her, and she smiled back.

"My name is Maria," she told him.

José stuttered, bowed awkwardly, and said, "José." At least he had remembered his name.

"Lisa is my cousin," Maria said, glancing toward the girl cutting the cake. "Her mother and my Dad are sister and brother."

José was clumsy at small talk. He thought for a second before saying that it was a nice party.

"Yes," Maria agreed. Then she moved away, perhaps looking for someone easier to talk to.

Living in East L.A. had its pros and cons. In the 1980s, Boyle Heights was a close-knit community. People looked out for one another. That was important, because the area was a battleground for competing gangs. Police helicopters patrolled it at night. The choppers seemed to circle overhead nonstop. Residents called them ghetto birds. There were drive-by shootings. A ten-year-old boy had been shot and killed a few years before José arrived. For the most part, though, the local cholos—recognizable in their pressed white tee shirts and khakis, their hair meticulously slicked back—left everyone else alone. The area was famous for its restaurants and bakeries. The main drag, Brooklyn Avenue, was lined by clothing and appliance stores, many owned by Jews who had first settled there before the great migrations from Mexico began. Many stayed behind even after the majority of the barrio's Jews had moved on to other neighborhoods in the city.

The best-known of its schools was Roosevelt High— named after Teddy not Franklin. Its football team was even called the Rough Riders. This is where José eventually enrolled. Roosevelt, with its teeming masses of students, was a far cry from Nava Sahagún. José learned English well enough to cope academically. But he still felt like an outsider.

José arrived in Boyle Heights almost twenty years after a turbulent period in the history of Roosevelt High. The school, like others in East L.A., had been caught up in a surge of racial consciousness. Tens of thousands of students had boycotted classes in the late 1960s to protest the inequality and racism in L.A. schools. The protests—dubbed "blowouts"— were led by a group called the Brown Berets, a Chicano version of the Black Panthers.

Something of this ferment lingered in the atmosphere of Roosevelt High, a sense of injustice perceived and challenged. José took it all in. However faint, he sniffed a whiff of activism in the air. It intrigued him. Even now, years later, it was an exciting smell.

One day between classes, José crossed paths with Maria in a school corridor.

"Hi," he said. "How are things?"

"They're good," she replied. "Yourself?"

"Okay. Listen: What are you doing after school today?"

Maria giggled. He was a little bolder than before. "That depends. What did you have in mind?"

"What would you say to a walk in the park? We could talk. You wouldn't be late getting home."

Maria considered the proposal. "That's good," she said. "But I have to get home on time."

José was gallant enough to buy Maria an ice cream cone from one of the ice cream trucks on 4th Street before moving on to Hollenbeck Park. The park was reputed to be the stomping ground for devil worshippers who performed animal sacrifice there at night. But the flowers were beautiful, the trees offered abundant shade, and the park wasn't crowded. So this was where he took Maria. It was his first date in his new country.

"Do you like it here?" she asked him as they strolled along hand in hand.

"It's all right," he confessed.

"Think you'll ever go back?"

José licked his ice cream before replying: "To visit maybe. My mother still lives in San Judas."

"The crime doesn't bother you here?"

José snorted. "Remember where I come from," he said.

"The gangs are not all bad," Maria said. "One time my kid brother had a bike accident. He was barefoot, and one of the cholos carried him home. Another cholo brought the bike back later that day. That's pretty good, *verdad*?"

Maria was a petite girl, with curly black hair held in check by a ruby-red headband. When she was thinking about something, she would fuss with strands of hair that escaped from the headband. Her family was conservative and would have liked Maria to dress like a convent girl. But she had an independent streak, as well as a fashion sense, and dressed in Jordache jeans and Reeboks. She had a dazzling smile. Her hands were delicate. Her nails were carefully manicured.

José would have liked to rub up against her Jordache jeans, but he was careful not to push his luck.

"What will you do after Roosevelt?" Maria asked him.

"College if I can manage it. Anyway, that's years from now. I'll need to earn some money first."

"Interested in summer work? *Mi padre* runs a construction company. He's always looking for summer workers. What do you think?"

José weighed the collateral advantages of working for Maria's Dad. He mumbled something noncommittal.

"I'll ask him if you want," Maria volunteered.

José said, "Thanks," and smiled at her.

Is that how things worked here, he wondered. Everything seemed to depend on who you knew. Tio Antonio, Maria. Everything was done through contacts. José began to feel as if the tide had turned. It was now running in his favor.

LOS CAMINOS REALES

The land or the roads: Which was the most valuable? The roads probably. And the railroads. Let's not forget about the railroads. Without the roads and the railroads, the land wouldn't be worth pig shit. But what would the roads *or* the railroads *or* the land be worth without water? Water was the key to everything else. That was the secular trinity, a triad of NAFTA-related development: land, transport, and water.

The master plan called for the El Paso-Juárez metro region to be turned into a transportation hub, a concrete and steel spider's web of highways and rail lines. First a ring road around El Paso; then a road to link downtown Juárez with its western suburbs like San Judas; finally, a forty-mile rail spur to start south of Juárez, pass west of the city, then cross the Rio Grande to a spanking new Union Pacific facility on the U.S. side of the border. And the centerpiece of all this construction frenzy was the road south from New Mexico across the Rio Grande, shooting straight arrow through the heart of San Judas. This was the mother of all roads, targeting the biggest of all the maquiladoras in Juárez, the giant Fox-Conn plant, and from there thrusting like a dagger into the breast of the Chihuahua desert.

The plan smelled of money. A pigsty full of money! The infrastructure involved in these schemes included $150 million for the Union Pacific terminal, projected to handle one hundred thousand container cars a year. The state of New Mexico agreed to build a connecting road to the facility for $5 million. And the Mexican spur, which hooked up with the Union Pacific terminal, had a price tag of $40 million.

Of course, the owners of the land over which these roads and railroads passed stood to gain handsomely. The road through San Judas, for example, would go to a port of entry (POE) on the border. The crossing, five traffic lanes to a side, was expected to process between ten and twenty thousand vehicles a day. Each of these vehicles would be paying a toll. That volume of traffic would also benefit a casino conveniently located on the American side of the port. In 2006, the general manager of that casino pledged to contribute $12 million over three years to bring the port of entry to completion.

The Mexican railroad spur ran past a plot of land belonging to one of Mexico's richest men, Eloy Vallina. Eloy was the eldest of nine children. In May 1960, Vallina's father was murdered. The killer? None other than the chief of police of Chihuahua— the father of the woman Vallina was said to be having an affair with. The chief gunned Vallina down on the doorstep of his own bank; he was subsequently sentenced to fifteen years in prison for this crime of honor.

Eloy fils assumed the presidency of the family's Banco Comercial Mexicano. When his bank was nationalized in

1982, Vallina told a Mexican publication, "They took my bank from me, so I shall take Chihuahua from them."

The Vallina family had a multitude of business interests in Chihuahua. From the 1940s onward, it engaged in logging ventures in a region of Chihuahua called the Sierra Tarahumara. (This is the region known to Americans as Copper Canyon.) Their company, Grupo Industrial Bosques de Chihuahua—known more simply as El Grupo—grew out of Banco Comercial Mexicano. El Grupo was the largest of the companies logging in Tarahumara. By the early 1960s, El Grupo employed six thousand workers. Twenty-five years later, that figure had mushroomed to twenty-four thousand.

The family came under fire from environmentalists for its role in the deforestation of the Sierra Tarahumara. A survey in 1965, by which time logging was being carried out on a commercial scale, revealed that companies were blithely ignoring limits on extraction and slashing indiscriminately the most desirable stands of trees. Lumberjacks had poached timber on land specifically allocated to an indigenous community, sawing the choicest timber and leaving behind a wasteland prone to erosion. Local officials chose to ignore these transgressions and covered them up by filing bogus management plans.

Changes to the Mexican Constitution in the 1990s eliminated land redistribution to peasants. These reflected the impact of Mexico's participation in NAFTA. Lumber extraction increased. By 1997, less than 2 percent of the country's old-growth pine and oak forests—which had originally covered 93,560 square kilometers of Mexico—were left standing. Something like half of the country's forests vanished in the twentieth century alone.

Companies gained access to the timber of the Sierra Tarahumara through rental agreements that were patently unfavorable to the indigenous inhabitants of the region. This, of course, stoked resentment on the part of the inhabitants of the Sierra.

"Even though the land no longer belongs to us, don't we belong to it?" cried one village elder. "We are the children of this land, and as children we have a greater right than some big shot who can remove its timber just because he has money."

The plot of land that Eloy Vallina owned on the border, a fraction of his holdings in the Tarahumara—it measured forty-nine thousand acres—was still more than twice the size of the island of Manhattan. Vallina bought it in 1998 for approximately $5 million. Days before leaving office in 2004, the governor of Chihuahua, whose campaign Vallina had supported, expropriated 212 hectares of Vallina's land (a bit less than 524 acres) for $4.6 million. That left Vallina with his original land purchase largely intact, for which he had paid, in effect, less than $10 per acre.

Vallina became chairman of a Mexican holding company that ultimately acquired a company called Elamex. Elamex managed a number of maquiladoras. Shares in the company were sold on NASDAQ starting in 1995. At that time, with seventeen manufacturing facilities in Mexico, it was ranked the fifth largest maquila operator in Mexico. It was delisted from the NASAQ in 2006.

What did Vallina hope to do with his land on the U.S./Chihuahua border?

The plan was to create a mirror image of what was projected to take place on the U.S. side of the border. Developers aimed to create a strip of land slated for industrial use, stretching from the Pacific Ocean to the Gulf of Mexico. They would proceed to stud it with maquiladoras, workers' dormitories, and malls to supply the needs of people living there.

"Whether the country likes it or not, the manufacturing platform of the U.S. is going to be on the Mexican border."

The man who let slip that judgment, the man whose vision was to transform the border area between the U.S. and Mexico into an industrial hub, was William Sanders— "Billy" to his cronies—a real estate developer who was born in El Paso. He had gone on to make a fortune in the Chicago real estate management business. The son of an advertising agency owner, Billy enjoyed a middle-class childhood in El Paso that included selling Coca-Colas to golfers at the thirteenth hole of the El Paso Country Club. Sanders showed initiative at an early age. In high school, he operated a landscape business. This led to a stint at Cornell University, where he earned an undergraduate degree in agriculture and life sciences. Young Billy then launched a successful career in real estate development. A canny sense of when to cash in his chips before things went south made Sanders a very wealthy man. One example was a real estate holding company in Santa Fe, NM, which Sanders founded and sold at the end of 2002 for an estimated $5.4 billion.

At that time, *Businessweek* called him the most powerful landlord in the country.

In December 2003, Sanders started yet another real estate company, the Verde Group, which invested in binational projects along the border. These included maquiladoras. We need to throw one more name into Sanders's lucrative batch of holdings. The developer cofounded a coalition of business types from both sides of the border— bankers, media owners, and politicians. This one was called the Paso del Norte Group (PDNG).

"His business model in land speculation has been to raise the expectations of his project and then to sell them to third parties before conclusion, sometimes, even before starting them." This was how one consultant for a binational border development assessed Sanders's secret for success.

One property that Sanders did not sell was his 125-square mile ranch near Columbus, New Mexico. This, one should remember, was the site of Pancho Villa's most daring and notorious raid during the Mexican Revolution. The Verde Group lost no time in purchasing a sizeable chunk of land surrounding the site for the International POE and lying astride the road leading from the U.S. south into the colonia of San Judas.

"The border is such a powerful generator of value," Sanders told one reporter. (He gave few interviews. This was one of them.) "The United States is the largest consumer market in the world and the most efficient place in the world to produce those goods is on the U.S.-Mexican border."

The mayor of El Paso asked Sanders to redevelop the city's downtown. Over the years, the area had sunk into a state of dereliction. "The biggest failure that I know of in the United States is El Paso," the developer once said. Sanders culled ideas from his stint in Chicago, where he had been a member of the Commercial Club, an organization that tried to discreetly guide the city's development. The Downtown Plan that Sanders eventually proposed for El Paso was introduced by the group that he had helped found, the PDNG.

From the get-go, the PDNG generated suspicion. Its membership, which was by invitation only, remained a closely guarded secret. The group preferred to work behind closed doors. Eventually the group was pressured to divulge the identity of its members. The disclosure revealed a bevy of well-connected heavy hitters from El Paso and Ciudad Juárez.

The principal bone of contention that critics picked with the plan was its objectives for the city's Second Ward. This was the Segundo Barrio, El Paso's most history-packed neighborhood. Thousands of Mexicans escaping the revolutionary chaos of their homeland had crossed through the barrio. It was the first stop on an underground railroad that stretched all the way through the Southwest into the Great Plains and

California. Lucy Carrillo, the Mother Courage of San Judas, the woman who had arranged meals for Hands Across the Border, had taken this route on her escape to Los Angeles.

And there was the barrio's roll call of famous residents. This is where Pancho Villa came to lick scoops of ice cream and to sleep with his wife, where Francisco Madero engineered the overthrow of the dictator Porfirio Diaz during the Mexican Revolution of 1910, and where Victoriano Huerta, the drunkard who plotted the assassination of Madero and the overthrow of his government, died of cirrhosis of the liver, his bed positioned so that he was facing Mexico when he drew his last breath. The Segundo was where the saintly Teresa Urrea, who could miraculously heal the sick, sought refuge after being forced out of Mexico; where Mariano Azuela published his novel about the Revolution, *Los de Abajo*; where Sylvestre Terrazas published his own newspaper, editorializing about labor movements and exhorting his countrymen to remain loyal to the motherland; and where Henry Flipper, the first African-American graduate of West Point, who played a prominent role in the 1920s Teapot Dome scandal, had lived. They had all passed through at one time or another. Now only their ghosts lingered on.

Those ghosts did not lack for live company that made a lot more noise than they did: during the day, shoppers thronged the district's two principal thoroughfares—El Paso Street and Stanton Street. Consumers bustled in and out of shops that sold everything from caged canaries to guitars to skintight jeans, the latter displayed on rows of half-body mannequins, their pert fannies thrust out toward the roadway.

The PDNG plan called for a gentrification of the Segundo Barrio. It envisioned beautifully scrubbed facades and leafy esplanades, coffee shops, and toney restaurants. This required the demolition of some buildings—it was unclear which ones—and their replacement by condos, parking garages, even big-box stores that would certainly have spelled the doom of the mom-and-pop shops in the neighborhood.

To promote the project, the city funded an ad campaign that included a representation of an old cowpoke and the caption "male, 50-60 years old, gritty, dirty, lazy, speak(s) Spanish and is uneducated." The image ran in juxtaposition with photos of Penelope Cruz and Matthew McConaughey, avatars of the beautiful people who presumably would flock to El Paso once the bulldozers had done their level best. Who could find fault with that? Those who found the ad offensive were just shiftless paisanos whom Bill Sanders and his partners were trying to evict.

The area would be "de-Mexicanized," according to a blunt observer, one not squeamish about his choice of words. The instrument of transformation—one that stuck in the craw of those who opposed the development—was the threat of eminent domain, not between private owners and government but between the current owners of property in the barrio and the developers. Opponents argued that such a use of eminent domain violated Texas law. That did not seem to deter backers of the Downtown Plan.

If "we weren't able to work something out," said one of Sanders's associates, city officials would have to "begin the process of taking their property." At fair market value, of course.

It was the largest land grab in the recent history of Texas, said one lawyer representing a group of downtown businessmen. Opposition to the deal coalesced around an organization called Paso del Sur. Father Joe had a hand in its inception. Its web page was a sort of bulletin board for opinions both pro and con the proposed development. Mostly con. People associated with the neighborhood in one way or another spoke out to oppose the PDNG plan.

"This does not pass my smell test," said Paul Moreno, a state representative who had grown up in the Segundo

Barrio. "It's too heavily slanted toward a few wealthy families in El Paso."

In the face of unrelenting pressure from the opposition, the El Paso City Council decided in the summer of 2006 to prohibit the use of eminent domain for the plan. We should add an important footnote in this episode of El Paso history: Bill Sanders's son-in-law Beto O'Rourke served on the city council at this time. It's worth noting that O'Rourke distanced himself from racist promotion for the redevelopment plan like the one presented in the Cruz-McConaughey ad. "Beto does not approve of that kind of language to describe those in his community," said his spokesman. A charismatic politician, O'Rourke went on to serve three terms in Congress before challenging Ted Cruz (R-TX) for his Senate seat. He came within a whisker of defeating the incumbent. Beto, who is universally known by his Spanish nickname, then made a run for the presidency, which the media lost no time in lavishing attention on.

The Downtown Plan was eventually shelved to be replaced by another one that was more expansive. This new proposal encompassed the whole city. It was called Plan El Paso.

The PDNG climbed on board, and all seemed to be going well until developers announced that the plan involved the erection of a sports stadium, to be built on the site of the city hall. To make room for the arena, the El Paso city hall, which was less than forty years old, would have to be blown up. Old suspicions about the motives of the PDNG resurfaced. Nonetheless, voters approved overwhelmingly the $225 million bond issue floated to finance the new construction, and the "old" city hall disappeared in a cloud of dynamite-induced dust on April 14, 2013.

PDNG offered an example of the chumminess of the big players on the Texas-New Mexico-Chihuahua border. For example: Eloy Vallina Garza, the son of Eloy Vallina Laguera,

was a member of PDNG (as was Sanders, of course); Eloy
Vallina Laguera himself was on the board of the Verde
Group (as, of course, was Sanders); the elder Vallina and
Pablo Schmidt both sat on the New Mexico-Chihuahua
Commission for Binational Development; Pablo's mother,
Doña Patricia, joined the Strategic Plan for Ciudad Juárez,
to which she contributed financial support.

Membership on these boards gave developers knowledge of what was coming down the pike. This was as good
as money in the bank. It allowed them to influence how projects were hatched in a way that could be advantageous to
their own interests. There was nothing illegal about this. It
was just the way things were done. And this was how the rich
got richer and the poor were ignored or manipulated.

Not land but water was the most precious commodity
in the Southwest. Without water, much of the land would
be worthless. The land that Eloy Vallina owned on the
Mexican side of the border lay atop an aquifer known as
Conejos Médanos—Rabbit Dunes in Spanish. The governor
of Chihuahua announced plans to drill two dozen wells into
the aquifer and to build a pipeline to supply Ciudad Juárez
with water. The pipeline was to be constructed by a company
belonging to Mexico's wealthiest man, Carlos Slim, who was
understood to be sinking $100 million into the project. In
return, he wrung a concession out of Ciudad Juárez to sell
water to the municipality for a decade. The pipeline would
cross land owned by Vallina, together with San Judas, which
the Schmidt family claimed.

On the U.S. side of the border, one big water issue
wound up in court. Bill Sanders's company, Verde Real Estate,
undertook negotiations in the fall of 2003 to buy nineteen
thousand acres of land opposite Eloy Vallina's property in
Mexico. At the same time, Sanders's reps sought to acquire
the water rights then owned by a bankrupt developer and
to work out an agreement with Doña Ana County in New

Mexico, where the land was located, to secure permission to dispose of waste water.

Sanders's co-chairman for the Verde Group, Ron Blankenship, explained it this way: "Everything has to work together. We don't buy the land if we don't have the water rights."

The water rights permit that Verde aimed to procure was unprecedented in its magnitude. For starters, all the water in the lower Rio Grande Basin had already been appropriated. New Mexico routinely turned down requests for new permits. With each passing year, the water situation in the Rio Grande Valley had grown ever more dire. In the summer of 2003, it was actually necessary to irrigate the Rio Grande because the river had dried up so much. Climatologists reckoned that by the halfway point of the new century, the median streamflow of the Rio Grande would decrease by 13 percent. By the end of the century, they predicted that the river would lose 30 percent of its water.

Nevertheless, the bankruptcy judge approved the sale of the water rights. Under the terms of the agreement, Verde paid $6.4 million for the right to pump twelve thousand acre-feet and to hold in reserve an additional two thousand acre-feet for nine years. (An acre-foot is the volume of an acre one foot deep.) Doña Ana County—which was Verde's partner in the proceedings and the county where Verde owned its land on the U.S. side of the border—obtained the right to four to six thousand acre-feet of water.

On the Mexican side of the border, matters proceeded on a parallel track. In December 2005, the mayor of Ciudad Juárez called a meeting ostensibly to discuss (actually, to rubber-stamp) the project to sink wells in the Rabbit Dunes and pipe the water to Ciudad Juárez. Four dozen protestors carrying balloons and posters attended the meeting. An even larger number of the mayor's people—let's call them the Rabbiteers—were there, as well. As the evening wore on, things got noisy, and the city councilors decided to vacate the chamber to continue their deliberations in a private chamber. The Rabbiteers started to chant the mayor's nickname: "*Teto! Teto!*" The mayor grinned. He turned his thumb up, then he turned it down. That gesture doomed the protestors. As soon as he had left the chamber, the Rabbiteers began shoving and pushing the anti-Dunes protestors, which included people of the cloth—priests and nuns—and teachers.

"They started kicking us, hitting us, knocking us down," one of the anti-Dunes people said later. "The police were there. They didn't do anything. They just watched."

A petition drive mounted by the anti-Dunes faction collected more than fifty thousand signatures. It failed because city officials invalidated a large number of signatures.

Eloy Vallina had the last word, which the press naively attributed to a guilty conscience: "*La corrupción somos todos, nadie se salva.*" We are all corrupt. There are no exceptions.

CONFLICT

Father Joe had been present at the municipal meeting to discuss the pipeline project from the Rabbit Dunes aquifer to Ciudad Juárez. He and José Bernal had gone together. Like other protestors there, they had both sustained injuries during the brawl that broke out at the end of the meeting. Father Joe's injuries had been slight: a grazed shin, some black and blue marks on his right arm, a scratch on his left cheek. José got a black eye and a ripped shirt. Father Joe had tried to restrain Ojos del Lobo from mixing it up with the thugs all around them, grabbing him by the collar and pulling him away from the pro-development faction. That, in fact, was how the priest had been hurt. The more lasting damage for both men was psychological: How could this happen in a civic function? Under the noses of the cops who ringed the chamber?

When Padre Borelli got home that night—he was then staying in the shack in front of Casa Amistad that belonged to the Spiritan Order—he had some things to mull over. What most perplexed and annoyed him was the vacant look in the eyes of the police officers and their utterly impassive faces. They looked as if they had all undergone lobotomies. Or were they doing drugs?

Since the beginning of the confrontation between the Schmidt family and the settlers in San Judas, José Bernal had taken to spending more and more time in the neighborhood, staying with friends and family—distant cousins for the most part, since his own parents, first his father, then, years later, his mother, had passed away—and returning to the U.S. infrequently to work on construction projects in California where he had gone to high school and college.

Like many Mexicans who lived near the U.S. border, José was truly bilingual, fluent in both English and Spanish. His plan was to settle down in the U.S. His ex-girlfriend's father in Los Angeles had been his boss in the construction business. This was the man who had opened doors for José at the beginning of his career. Then the troubles blew up in San Judas. José felt that to leave would be an act of betrayal to kith and kin. So he stayed on. Although he was reserved by nature, he grew more involved in the settlers' struggle. He developed a close friendship with Father Joe, and he began to read newspapers like *La Jornada*. Before his departure to the U.S., he had not known the periodical even existed.

The Schmidt family had staked out a claim to much of San Judas. Was it a valid claim? Pablo's father Emanuel had bought the land from a speculator in the 1960s, or so Pablo asserted. At that time, he claimed, the only living creatures in San Judas were rabbits and rattlesnakes. The purported sale predated the declaration by President Echeverria that the region to the west of Ciudad Juárez, which included San Judas, was federal property where settlers were free to take possession of plots of land, build homes, raise crops, and pasture animals.

The Schmidts went further: they denied that settlement in the area started in 1970. In their version of events, squatters began arriving after that date. Sensing a problem in the making, Emanuel Schmidt had given four hundred acres (or so the family insisted) to the man he identified as the leader of the squatters. This "gift" came with the stipulation that the squatters stay within that parcel of land. It didn't work. The squatters sold off the four hundred acres to settlers, who each took five acres, fenced off what they believed was their land, and began to build on it.

As his father's sole heir, Pablo still owned over half the colonia of San Judas, or so he argued. Pablo was able to produce a title to the land, but it was adjudged to be a fake by critics who said that the "seller" did not actually own the land the Schmidt family claimed to have bought from him. It was more than a coincidence, critics—including the settlers in San Judas—observed, that Pablo Schmidt began to press his claim only when it became apparent that the land was strategically valuable. The Mexican government had invited claimants to property in San Judas to come forward to challenge the president's decree in 1975. Why hadn't Doña Patricia Schmidt done something then?

The Schmidt clan began to tighten the screws on the residents of the colonia. First, they disrupted the neighborhood's water supply by preventing water trucks from entering the neighborhood. It was a cruel irony that the water tower that serviced the area to the west of Ciudad Juárez rose on a hillside overlooking San Judas. "The water passes right in front of my house, but I can't get any," lamented one resident.

Next came the electricity. Rumors circulated in the colonia during the summer of 2002 that Pablo would try to cut their electricity off. This was a service that had only recently been established. Father Joe tried to calm people's fears. He assured them that the Federal Electric Commission (CFE were its initials in Spanish) would not undo what it had just put in place.

He was wrong. The Federal Electric Commission issued a statement that it "had made a mistake." Early one morning in September, the CFE sent a convoy of trucks to San Judas to uproot the electric poles in the barrio. Residents were waiting for them. Piling tires at the entrance to the barrio, they doused them with kerosene and set them alight. Faced with fire and the odor of incinerated rubber, the men from the CFE were not about to proceed. They vowed to return only with a police escort. The trucks from the CFE reversed and sped back down the mesa, swallowed up in clouds of dust. The men of San Judas cheered.

Their celebration was premature. In the spring of 2003, tension in San Judas jumped several notches when Pablo Schmidt sent in a gang of private guards—*un grupo de choque*—also identified as "White Guards" to make trouble for the settlers. The White Guards were thugs, but not run-of-the-mill cholos, recruited from the masses of unemployed youths milling about in the poor neighborhoods of west Juárez. No, these thugs were something special. They had a name: Mara Salvatrucha, sometimes called MS-13, the "13" because M is the thirteenth letter in the alphabet. The group originated not in Mexico but in the U.S., in Los Angeles to be precise, where it first arose to defend the Salvadoran community.

The group's initial motivation may have been noble, but MS-13 evolved into something decidedly more sinister as it spread beyond L.A. back into El Salvador, then Honduras, then into Mexico, where members were recruited by one drug cartel to kill workers for a rival cartel. The vigilantes morphed into criminals of a particularly repugnant stripe, elaborately tattooed mercenaries.

MS-13 gained notoriety for its cruelty, its pitiless revenge on double-crossing squealers who talked to the cops. There were so many knives stuck in the body of one turncoat MS member—ghoulishly photographed and disseminated on the web—that he looked like a human pincushion. These were the choir boys Pablo Schmidt brought in to "protect" the family's property in San Judas. They showed up early one morning in May 2003 armed with plastic pipes, clubs, even pistols: 9mm handguns and expensive Smith & Wesson models. The residents of San Judas complained about the firepower, but the mayor of Ciudad Juárez claimed that he was powerless to do anything about that, because the lads of MS-13 had gun permits.

What were the colonos to do? They met to plan for their mutual defense. They started to acquire an arsenal of primitive weapons. Fifty yards away, the cholos from MS-13 strutted in the street. They slapped their plastic pipes in their hands and taunted the settlers. They grinned broadly and made the tattoos on their pecs shimmy like Jell-O.

"We're here to have a go at them," bragged one of the thugs. "Let's see what these *maricones* can do against us."

The settlers reacted by marching on city hall to demand the removal of the MS-13. Surprisingly they were successful: just before retiring from office, the mayor of Ciudad Juárez declared that San Judas was "under siege." He ordered the arrest of the MS-13 members patrolling the neighborhood. Police hauled the punks off to jail. The settlers cheered.

But once again, their victory was short-lived. The CFE reissued its demand that electricity to the barrio be cut off. This time, when the crews from the CFE arrived to do their dirty work, they arrived with a police escort. By the end of the day, under the helpless gaze of the inhabitants of the district, the CFE crews toppled eighty electric poles. They loaded a dozen transformers on trucks. They dismantled five kilometers of high-tension wire. They coiled the wire on the ground like a dead snake. Then they hoisted it onto the beds of idling trucks. Finally, they hauled everything away. That night, San Judas, at least that part of the neighborhood coveted by the Schmidt clan, was as dark as the surrounding desert. The next day neither the whirring of ancient fans nor the wheezing of asthmatic refrigerators broke the silence of the barrio. What you heard was animal noises—the clucking of chickens, the forlorn grunting of swine—muffled by the heat of the summer sun.

Nor had the residents of San Judas seen the last of MS-13. In the spring of 2004, the goons were back. This time they brought construction material and equipment. Their first objective was to establish a semi-permanent camp just outside the neighborhood. This meant a cluster of small huts with a shared electric generator and portable toilets. A more menacing construction project, however, was on their agenda. Starting in the middle of the night, the Schmidts' White Guards erected a barbed-wire fence around the barrio. Concrete posts held the wire in place. This one gesture made a big chunk of San Judas into a concentration camp. No one could enter or leave without the White Guards' consent. That included supply trucks and city buses. Buses transporting women back from their work at the maquilas now stopped at the gate manned by MS-13 guards. From there, the women groped their way home in the dark.

Casa Amistad and Father Joe's shack (like the house of the ex-nuns Elvia Villalobos and Lina Sarlat) lay outside the perimeter of the enclosure. But Father Joe's chapel, the neighborhood's primary school, and the Sisters of Charity's clinic, as well as many houses, including Lucy Carrillo's, were sealed up behind the Berlin Wall of San Judas. Evaristo's and Lara's *tienda de abarrotes* likewise lay inside the enclosed area.

Inhabitants of San Judas, now prisoners in their own neighborhood, tried to tear the barbed-wire fence down. But the cholos from MS-13 took to hurling rocks at them. The cholos feigned charges with unsheathed knives. The police, in the meantime, stood by, passively observing the gathering rumble. Father Joe rushed to the scene of the confrontation. He thought back to the imbroglio at the municipal meeting in which he and several others had been hurt. He saw that a number of the colonos had bloody gashes on their arms and faces where the rocks had struck them.

"What's happening here? Why are you throwing rocks at these people?" the priest asked the White Guards.

The MS-13 eyed him sullenly. Their fists closed around the rocks they had not hurled. But they were forced to respect a man of God. A couple of them muttered "maricones" under their breath. The settlers, who loved and revered their padre, kept their silence although a few grunted their appreciation of his intervention. To these men, Father Joe said, "Stay calm. They are only doing what they have been ordered to do."

It took a measure of persuasion, but eventually Father Joe was able to defuse the situation. The settlers backed away from their MS-13 antagonists.

The authorities offered no real help to the colonos in their struggle. For example, the director of the Housing Authority advised the settlers to accept a Schmidt family offer of free land to resettle the colonos. That included free construction material. If the settlers lost their court battle, the director of the Housing Authority pointed out, they would lose everything.

One small and ultimately unfruitful victory did come the way of the settlers. The Federal Consumer Protection Agency ordered the CFE to restore electricity to the barrio. If that were not possible, then the settlers should be reimbursed for what they had spent to have electricity installed in San Judas in the first place.

"It is unheard of and inhuman to strip the electric services to a neighborhood where there are children, elderly, and sick, without first ordering an evacuation," cried a lawyer representing the colonos.

On the opposing side, the lawyer representing Pablo Schmidt was a pudgy man named Carlos Banda. He looked like an evil teddy bear. He wore granny glasses and impeccably laundered white shirts. His reaction to the court decision to restore electricity to San Judas oozed contempt. Restore the electric poles? "I'll put back five hundred," he sneered, "or as many as you want."

Things had come to such a pass that Father Joe took pen in hand and wrote an appeal to Pablo Schmidt that appeared in *El Diario*. "Stop the injustice," he lectured him. "Live according to your Christian faith. Think about your own charities in Ciudad Juárez and the good causes that you support. Unite with the families of San Judas to demonstrate your values, rather than erecting a barbed-wire fence like the ones in Nazi Germany."

The Schmidt clan was careful to stay in the background while hostilities raged. Rarely did they venture out of the compound of mansions where they resided in an elegant quarter of Juárez. But their influence on the conduct of the battle was never in doubt. One evening in the fall of 2004, a couple of trucks carrying Mara Salvatrucha men roared up to the chapel where Father Joe was accustomed to saying mass on Sundays. A man on horseback accompanied the trucks. He was later identified as Carlos Banda. The men fired shots and warned neighbors not to come close to the chapel. The intruders left but the trucks came back later that night with thugs armed with crowbars and sledgehammers. They jumped out and began demolishing the chapel. Within an hour, there was nothing left of Jesus de Nazareth but a jumble of splintered beams and broken glass.

Father Joe could not at first believe that men who were nominally Catholic would destroy a church. But his eyes disabused him of that naive belief.

"They are trying to demoralize us," he said to his parishioners. "It won't work. This Saturday we shall raise our church again, and Sunday we'll have mass there."

Good as his word, Father Joe celebrated mass the following Sunday in a new chapel constructed of adobe. Two hundred worshippers attended.

The Bishop of Juárez saw fit to condemn the destruction of the old chapel: "In pagan eyes, this was a small and insignificant place. But even a humble chapel is like a great cathedral in the presence of Christ. Those who destroyed it have committed an unspeakable sacrilege."

Would the bishop raise the issue with the Schmidt family, journalists asked him. That apparently was a different matter. "I wouldn't know what kind of dialogue to engage in with them," he said to the stupefaction of his interviewers. It was up to the authorities to investigate the matter and to resolve the problem. The bishop went on to unfurl the banner of Church dignity: "I am responsible for all matters dealing with the diocese of Ciudad Juárez, and I will support the authorities in whatever way I can."

MS-13 retired to their camp, at least for the time being. There they kept the settlers under surveillance, spying on them with binoculars. Some of the thugs had taken to wearing fake leather jackets unzipped to show off the tattoos on their pecs and abs. The back of each jacket pictured the head of a tiger with bared fangs. When Mara Salvatrucha ventured into San Judas, it was to attack the settlers, singling out leaders of the resistance for special treatment.

One of these confrontations occurred between one of the MS-13 hoods and José Bernal. He was now prominent in the demos mounted to protest Pablo Schmidt's walling off of San Judas. Angry words precipitated a shoving match between the two men. The hood pulled his gun and poked it in José's chest. José's grey eyes showed no fear. His face betrayed no emotion of any kind. But he threw up his hands in a gesture of surrender and backed off. After some grumbling and the customary barrage of insults, the set-to petered out. Like so many others, it would live on as only one of the barrio's history of hostile encounters.

Another more serious clash erupted at a gas distribution center near San Judas. A couple of MS-13 thugs ambushed a settler named David González. They beat him about the head and body with a baseball bat. The attack was so grievous that González was confined to a wheelchair for several days. This is how he arrived at the Ciudad Juárez police department, accompanied by friends and family, to press charges against the men who had beat him. The settlers were told that the police chief could not take action until they had spoken directly to Carlos Banda, the Schmidt family's representative.

Several weeks later. José Bernal spotted Carlos Banda in a street of San Judas. He accosted the lawyer in a non-threatening manner: "Why are you doing this?" he asked. "God is going to punish you for what you've done."

Banda scoffed: "By the time your God gets to me, I will have done what I have to do."

Banda was in San Judas to direct the demolition of an apparently abandoned house. A bus driver who lived in San Judas with his family drove past at that point. His name was Luis Guerrero. He rolled down the window of his truck and yelled at Banda: "Son of a bitch! Leave us alone."

Banda lost his cool. He turned to the men of his demolition crew and screamed, "Let the motherfucker have it!"

Banda's men dragged Luis Guerrero out of his truck and began beating him with anything that lay at hand: pipes, shovels, pickaxes. They hollered as they worked him over. Guerrero offered no resistance. He sought only to protect his face and body. The skin on his hands was being shredded by the beating he was taking.

"It all happened in a blur," José Bernal recalled later. He raced back to his car, which was parked nearby and retrieved a gun from the glove compartment. It was a pistol that one of his friends had insisted on giving him. He crawled back across the hard scrabble earth and took cover behind a pile of debris. When Banda's men realized that José had a shooter, they opened fire on him. José took a bullet in the left leg. He could feel the bullet's sting. A trickle of blood coursed down the inside of his calf.

Now it was José's turn: he began shooting, first at Banda's men, then at Banda himself. He took careful, ever so careful, aim and pumped two slugs into the lawyer's belly. Banda's glasses slid off his nose. A rust-red stain spread over his immaculate white shirt. Globs of mucous-laced blood gushed from his mouth. When the demolition crew realized that their boss had been shot, they hustled him into one of their cars and spun off, spewing pebbles behind them.

Settlers took Guerrero and Bernal to a nearby hospital. José was released the same day. Guerrero's situation, however, was critical. He was suffering from internal bleeding. The pain was excruciating. The doctors said that further X-rays would be needed to determine the location and extent of his injuries. Despite the care he received, Guerrero died two days later.

"This is a tragedy no one expected," his wife cried. Never in his life had Luis Guerrero been in a fight.

Still the authorities refused to intervene. "We have asked for calm," said the mayor. "But we are not judges."

What are you, *Señor el Alcalde*? said Father Joe to himself when he found out what had happened and what the mayor had said. Was the mayor no more than a lackey of rich businessmen?

Pablo Schmidt asserted that while doing their work his men had been roughed up by a small group of drunken settlers. Carlos Banda was alive, he said. That was all. Pablo gave no indication of his whereabouts.

In fact, Banda was never seen again. He vanished into thin air.

NOT THE CAVALRY BUT STILL SOMETHING

His was like the second coming. The people alongside his route saw not just a Zapatista leader. They saw Jesus on a motorbike. They saw the Messiah on a two-wheeled donkey. Subcomandante Marcos was driving across Mexico, across the Chihuahua desert into Ciudad Juárez.

He spoke everywhere to the people who lined his path. He spoke in parables and riddles that no one could make sense of but which everyone understood. At least they understood what he meant them to understood.

The initials EZLN for the Zapatista movement were painted in red across the handlebars of Sup Marcos's motorbike. He had named the motorbike *Sombraluz* (Shadow Light). The Zapatistas' penguin/genetically modified chicken rode behind Sup Marcos. The animal—whatever it was—squawked disconsolately and twisted its neck to gaze into the dust storm generated by the passage of the motorbike.

The Sup's odyssey across Mexico began in San Cristóbal twelve years to the day after the ragtag Zapatistas had seized that city in the 1994 uprising. Fifteen thousand supporters greeted his appearance ecstatically. "A new stage of the political struggle of the EZLN has arrived," proclaimed one of Marcos's comrades. "Delegate Zero (the Sup) will blaze the trail and open new doors."

"I have been chosen to go out across the country to test the road," said the Sup when his turn to speak came. The Zapatista movement was abandoning the armed struggle to try something different, "to reorganize the nation from below and to the left." The head of the country's Catholic Church approved. "It's a good thing," he said.

"We don't fear to die struggling," Marcos said. "The good word has already been planted in fertile soil, in the hearts of all of you, and it is there that Zapatista dignity will flourish."

Sombraluz hiccupped its way across Ciudad Juárez. Past the boarded-up shops of the center. Past the iron-grilled windows and bolted doors of houses. Past the burned-out street lights that lined the streets. Up to the border where street vendors were selling tamales and elotes and tacos to the men and women and flavored ice popsicles and licorice to the kids.

Marcos brought his bike to a halt. He dismounted in a haze of diesel fumes. The masked man wore a fraying army cap with a star emblazoned above the visor. He walked halfway across the Stanton Street Bridge. Troopers had blocked the bridge at both ends, solely for this occasion. Marcos looked out over the hump in the roadway down into El Paso's Segundo Barrio. This was the neighborhood that Bill Sanders and his partners had sought to gentrify. It was now packed solid with fervent Zapatista supporters. They were standing shoulder to shoulder. Some were waving the

EZLN flag. The midday heat was suffocating. Sweat streamed down the faces of the people and dripped into their eyes.

Sup Marcos addressed the masses, just as the Son of Man had once spoken to the multitudes from some unidentified mountain top in Palestine two millennia before. But Marcos was speaking not from some mountain top but from the hump in the middle of the Stanton Street Bridge, on a day in early summer when the temperature had soared into the 90s Fahrenheit in the shade, and he spoke these words:

> La Otra Campaña proposes to cross to the other side of the frontier. That's how we answer the U.S. war of conquest and its attempt to convert Mexico into one more star on its flag. We plan to go the other way around: we shall cross the frontier when Mexico takes its rightful place in the world.

Marcos gestured to the now blocked bridge between Mexico and the U.S.:

> Let this be a symbol: we dedicate this closure to all those who have disappeared for political reasons. We have met with the committee of mothers of those in Juárez who have disappeared. They tell us of the pain of losing a son or a daughter. They tell us of their struggle.

He asked his audience to recall the concept of the war of conquest:

> With the Indians of Mexico, we're launching a reconquest. Before now, the armies came with horses, muskets, and canons. Today it's political parties with their laws and their flunkey politicians.

A Black Hawk helicopter from the border patrol roared overhead. Hearing Sup Marcos's words was difficult, but the helicopter could not drown out the passion of his speech. It could not quell the anger of his listeners.

La Otra Campaña considers the other side here as part of Mexico, as part of ourselves, the way our blood is part of ourselves, and our fight doesn't recognize this helicopter, it doesn't recognize this line, it doesn't recognize the flag waving above us. Comrades, there is no other side. Those on the other side are sitting in that helicopter, sitting in the White House, and sitting in the Presidential Palace of Mexico.

The crowd, numbering more than two thousand, went ballistic. "*Viva, Zapata!*" they roared.

Zapata was alive today, alive in Sup Marcos's words, alive in his presence and in his voice, alive in the response of those who heard him, a people of one blood, one heritage, one nation.

"What do we want?" he went on when the crowd had quieted down. "A Juárez where young people are not murdered, where their lives do not end at an international bridge. That is the fundamental challenge of La Otra Campaña. It doesn't matter what river they cross, be it the Rio Grande or some other that we are asked to accept, as if they were walls and not the fountain of life that they should be."

A student from the University of Texas at El Paso stretched over the crowd to shake Marcos's hand. "It's important to contact people struggling for a better world, to share with them our own struggles," she said. "What makes Marcos special is that he represents more than just himself."

Among the many young people in Marcos's audience was José Bernal. He listened intently to the Zapatista leader. His eyes squinted in the intense sunlight. He felt the sweat trickle down his spine and darken the center fold of his shirt. But José seemed not to feel the heat of the day. From time to time, he balanced on the toes of his construction shoes to see above the heads of the people in front of him. When Marcos appeared to have finished his remarks, José elbowed his way forward to shout at the Subcomandante, "What about the situation in San Judas? Do you know about it?"

Marcos had, in fact, been told something about the problem, but he frowned. He grew peevish and complained that he knew nothing of the struggle.

> Friend, forgive me for saying this, but I hear you talking about San Judas, and no one has had the courtesy to tell us what is going on there. And we have heard about other problems, and we didn't even know about those. If La Otra Campaña in Juárez doesn't let us know what is happening, then who will?

In response to this testy remark, José and his friends arranged a special audience for Marcos with settlers from San Judas. The meeting took place in Lucy Carrillo's tiny living room. While the colonos talked to the Sup, a crowd of silent neighbors stood vigil outside her cinder block house. They waited and sweltered under the early summer sun, not exchanging so much as a word among themselves, not even swatting away the flies that buzzed around their faces.

The colonos' tales of harassment and forced eviction from their homes offered Marcos another example of class exploitation. Marcos sympathized with the colonos. But what could he offer them by way of concrete help? He wasn't there to lead the resistance to the Schmidt family. Sup Marcos was, by choice, long on riddles and—by necessity—short on practical suggestions. But he had one piece of advice: "You need a lawyer," he said. "And I can put you in touch with one." The colonos had a lawyer, but there was distrust between them and him, and the lawyer would soon be leaving the scene of action in any case.

At long last the world was paying attention to what was happening on the western edge of Ciudad Juárez.

"Urgent Action," demanded *Amnesty International (AI)*. It cited an instance of harassment in San Judas: men on horseback had surrounded a resident of the barrio. It was, in fact, Manny, the gallant of Alfred Von Bachmayr's insulation project. He was returning from a meeting when the horsemen threatened to beat him up. As he walked home, another man in a pickup truck drove past and spat at him: "What the fuck were you doing in that meeting?" Manny knew that his daughter was waiting for him, alone in the house, and he did not want to pick a fight with any of the Schmidt goons. He smiled sheepishly and mumbled something noncommittal.

Amnesty International asked people to write the authorities. To say what?

- To protect the residents of San Judas.
- To order an impartial investigation into the attacks on them.
- To stop any attempt to drive people off their land.

AI also appended to the appeal addresses of the governor of Chihuahua, the Mexican minister of the interior, and the mayor of Ciudad Juárez.

Still, the Schmidt juggernaut ground on. Slowly but inexorably. It aimed to crush the colonia of San Judas, one house at a time. The neighborhood was disappearing, one street after another. Because the MS-13 stopped trucks from coming into the community, Evaristo and Lara could not stock their grocery store. The commercial suffocation of the neighborhood obliged them to close their shop and accept the family's offer of a small parcel of land a mile away. There they rebuilt their tienda de aberrotes with cinder block and metal sheeting. Other small shops in San Judas followed suit. San Judas was left without businesses of any sort. Within an hour of Evaristo and Lara's decamping, bulldozers screeched up to what had been their little grocery store and smashed down its walls, its roof, its two tiny windows with their ornamental grills. They overturned the begonias in coffee tins and splintered the shelves and display cases that now stood empty. Then they spread a thick layer of soil over what had been a home and a business, leaving no trace of human industry and habitation.

In the fall of 2008, a group of activists from Las Cruces, New Mexico, buttonholed the governor of the state, Bill Richardson, to ask him to intervene in the San Judas dispute. The governor promised to do what he could. The activists sought support online and supplied the email addresses of officials like the governor of the state of Chihuahua and a sample letter to anyone who would write the governor to ask for his intervention. A few days later, the same group interrupted Governor Richardson's tour of southern New Mexico, where he was stumping for local Democratic candidates, to urge him to do something about the situation on the border. Despite numerous entreaties over the previous year, the governor seemed not to recall the treatment of the colonos in San Judas, although Father Joe's allies in southern New Mexico had jammed the governor's phone lines with messages of support for the settlers for days on end. Activists gave him a packet of information about the atrocities at San Judas, including the murder of Luis Guerrero, the cutting off of electricity and water to the barrio, and the destruction of homes by the White Guards. The governor continued to go around glad-handing people in the audience. Then he made a brief speech before returning to the Las Cruces activists to admit that he now remembered hearing about the troubles on the border. In the heat of the current campaign, they must have slipped his mind.

"What do you want me to do?" the governor asked. "I want to do something more than just make a public statement about it."

Contact the governor of the state of Chihuahua, the activists urged him. And stop all binational projects until the rights of the residents of San Judas are respected. The problem arose directly from what developers were doing and were hoping to do around the proposed port of entry at Sunland Park. Settlers from San Judas had wanted to come and speak to Governor Richardson in person, and so he was told, but they were too scared to leave their homes for fear that the thugs of MS-13 might destroy them in their absence. Supporters in southern New Mexico made a request on their behalf for gallon jugs of water, flashlights and batteries, kerosene lamps, walkie-talkie radios, and cell phone chargers.

They had reason to be fearful. About the time the activists from Las Cruces were hounding Bill Richardson, a resident of San Judas was preparing to feed his animals. His name was Rafael Piñon. A squad of soldiers smashed their way into his house. They threw the seventy-three-year-old man against a wall. Piñon had an illegal firearm in his house, the soldiers said. Pablo Schmidt had tipped them off. Then the soldiers turned the place upside down and "found" a sack of marijuana and an automatic pistol.

"You brought that with you," Piñon stated.

This remark seemed to enrage the soldiers who threatened to shoot him.

"Go ahead," Piñon told them.

His courage gave the soldiers pause. "You've got guts," said their commanding officer.

The soldiers hustled Piñon into the rear of a truck, where they blindfolded him and kicked him in the ribs. The colono had no idea where they were taking him. He never did find out, either. The soldiers stripped him of his shoes and shirt. Then they released him in the desert outside Ciudad Juárez. Piñon limped back to the house where he had lived for thirty-five years. There he found that his nonfunctioning television and his mattress had been stolen.

Piñon pressed charges against the soldiers at the local police station. A few days afterward, the police asked him to come down to the station to reactivate his complaint. "When I got back home," he told a journalist covering the story, "I found that my house had been leveled and all my animals stolen."

Rafael Piñon had built his house with his own hands. He had kept four dozen hens, ten roosters, three hogs, and a slew of rabbits. Now they were all gone: house and livestock. Even the photographs of his children.

"All I had left were the clothes on my back," he wailed. "They knock down our houses and steal our animals, and then they go back to their camp and make a barbeque."

Piñon's property had been appraised at more than $20 thousand. Pablo Schmidt offered to buy it at a tenth of that price. That, in Raphael's words, "was a joke."

Rafael Piñon was a bitter man. He had thought about killing his tormentors, but, as a good Catholic, he could not bring himself to commit such a crime. Still . . . "Sometimes there are moments," he mumbled.

The North American Human Rights Delegation is an umbrella group comprising a number of U.S. organizations. These include the National Lawyers Guild and La Alianza Latinoamericana. The delegation spent a week in the Ciudad Juárez/El Paso region in the spring of 2008. It interviewed residents of San Judas and El Paso's Segundo Barrio and wrote a report on its findings. On one occasion, MS-13 denied members of the group access to the contested area on the pretext that they were not Mexican. (A week before the delegation visited the region, the same thugs had set upon a human rights official for the state of Chihuahua and beat him up. The man had been attempting to make an official inspection of the situation in the barrio.) After citing instances of outrageous behavior on the part of the Schmidt goons and the delinquency of civil authorities, the delegation concluded its report by observing that:

> Human rights violations are taking place against the residents of the neighborhood with the tacit consent

of the local government. The land development driving the displacement of residents is reflected in other areas of the immediate border region, including Segundo Barrio in El Paso, Texas. Rather than being isolated cases of displacement, the cases described in this report appear to be interconnected.

Raphael Piñon was not the only old man to be molested by the MS-13. There were other incidents. One involved a man of the same age as Piñon. His name was Cruz Reza. Everyone in San Judas called him Don Cruz. Before the troubles began, Don Cruz managed to get by selling the goats that he raised on his little farm. From time to time, his girlfriend would come up to San Judas to visit him. But with Mara Salvatrucha in control of the barbed-wire fence that surrounded the neighborhood, his girlfriend could no longer come and go as she pleased and Don Cruz could not get food for his goats.

"Sell the damn goats," the guards told him. "Sell them all. They don't belong to you, anyway."

For some reason, the thought that Don Cruz could sell his goats and keep the money angered the guards. They tied him up, hand and foot, and began slapping him around.

"Where the fuck is the money for the goats?" they demanded.

They told the army that Don Cruz was keeping a firearm in his house. Soldiers searched Don Cruz's house and found his .22 rifle.

"What the fuck do you want this for?" they asked him.

"To shoot hares and coyotes," Don Cruz answered. "Or thieves."

The soldiers confiscated the rifle. Don Cruz was left with less and less. His livestock was gone—once upon a time he had possessed 80 goats, 70 pigs, and 180 chickens. He found himself with a single sow—*una marrana*.

He was told that none of what he had lost belonged to him. It all belonged to the rightful owners of San Judas, the Schmidt family, who offered to purchase his property for fifty thousand pesos, less than $5 thousand.

Don Cruz began to live like a hermit. He never ventured out of his house for fear that the White Guards would take advantage of his absence to knock the shack down. Neighbors brought him food and news. Cruz Reza stayed in contact with the outside world with his cell phone. He recharged it with the battery of his pickup truck.

★

Put the Mexican state on trial!

That was how hundreds of people felt, people who gathered in Ciudad Juárez early in 2012 to meet representatives of the Permanent People's Tribunal (known by its initials in Spanish TPP). The reps from TPP had come to the city to hear firsthand of the abuses inflicted on the country since the last century.

The TPP was born in the summer of 1974. It was the successor of the Bertrand Russell War Crimes Tribunal, named after the British philosopher and political activist. That organization had burst upon the world's media stage when it exposed war crimes committed in Vietnam during the country's ten-year civil war. Since its birth, the TPP has examined scores of atrocities in a dozen countries. The tribunal agreed to set up a chapter in Mexico in response to a request filed by human rights groups.

"We have a duty to show what the reality is, and we will do so with complete independence." That was the comment of a French jurist who was also a member of the Mexico chapter of the TPP. He went on to say:

Mexico has a relatively good international human rights image, because it has signed all of the treaties

and conventions, and the role of the TPP will be to
demonstrate whether or not that image reflects reality.

The organization's verdicts were nonbinding, although
they were based on international law. "That's the idea of a
popular alternative justice that implies the defense of rights,"
said one Mexican member of the TPP. For Mexico, the
organization brought together eight judges. These included
the cofounder of Argentina's Mothers of the Plaza Cinco de
Mayo and the daughter of the revolutionary theorist Frantz
Fanon. The Mexican chapter of the TPP crisscrossed the
country collecting testimony. The group eventually incorporated into its findings all that it had documented. Those
findings were published in the fall of 2014.

Of course, the TPP delegation heard plenty about San
Judas and the neighborhood's fight with the Schmidt guards.
"For me, it's a good thing," one resident said, "because people
are coming together to find out what is happening over there
and to find out what is happening over here."

During its session in Ciudad Juárez, a convoy of Federal
Police trucks, packed with black-clad cops, masked and armed
to the teeth, circled the hall where the TPP was meeting.

Undeterred by the cops' show of muscle, a spokes-
woman for the Catholic Church labor ministry said, "This
tribunal represents a hope for justice that comes from the
people, from the testimonies of the people." Another local
activist told an American reporter that the TPP might start
a U.S. chapter, because "the U.S. is a source of terror as well
as a source of hope; there are many people in the U.S. who
are worried about what is going on in Mexico."

The final report of the TPP Mexico chapter came out in
the spring of 2015. How can one begin to describe its indict-
ment of criminal practices in the country? The word "scath-
ing" comes to mind. The authors opened their report with
the statement:

In this realm of impunity that is today's Mexico, there are murders with no murderers, torture with no torturers, sexual violence with no abusers, in a constant abdication of responsibility, in which it would seem that the thousands and thousands of massacres, murders, and systematic violations of the rights of peoples are always isolated acts or marginal situations, rather than true crimes for which the State bears responsibility.

The report condemned NAFTA, which it characterized as part of a "legal and political web of domination." (The report included a comment by the opinion editor of *La Jornada*, a previously cited newspaper: "Mexico is like just one more state of the United States but without their laws or rules.")

The TPP jurists put that remark in their assessment of the trade pact. Moreover, they said:

It is vital that we understand that NAFTA and the other neoliberal institutions are not designed to promote the social good.

A panel of TPP judges recommended that Mexico withdraw from NAFTA:

The economy can't be above the dignity of human life, and the free trade agreement has benefited only a few.

Page after page, the findings unveiled a litany of scandals. These included the femicides of Ciudad Juárez, environmental degradation, unsolved murders, the intimidation of the press, the muzzling of free speech, slave labor and torture, rape, and the flouting of trade union rights. One telling sentence included a clear reference to San Judas:

There are allegations of dwellings being destroyed to force families and communities to move in order to free up land for various industrial, mining, tourism, or road infrastructure projects.

While jurists inside were hearing of the land dispute in San Judas, residents of the colonia were outside the meeting hall, where they had set up a table to sell bottles of their locally produced salsa.

The TPP report appeared in the immediate aftermath of the abduction and murder of forty-three teacher trainee students in the town of Iguala in the south of the country. They were part of a group of one hundred students from a teachers' college—the Raúl Isidro Burgos Rural Teachers College of Ayotzinapa—not far from Mexico City. They had planned to protest what they considered to be discriminatory practices on the part of the government in hiring and funding projects. To start off, they commandeered a fleet of buses to take them to Iguala.

(This was not the first time that had happened: students routinely hijacked their means of transport. After the demonstration they attended was finished, the students routinely returned the buses. The bus company tolerated their behavior without complaint.)

The students' goal was to disrupt a meeting held to commemorate the public works undertaken by the wife of the mayor of Iguala. Their escapade started out as a lark. The students were happy and relaxed, chatting amiably with their drivers. Then local police intercepted the students en route, acting, one can reasonably assume, on orders from the mayor. They fired tear gas and punctured the buses' tires. "We're going to kill all of you," the cops yelled, according to one of the bus drivers. One cop thrust his pistol into the driver's chest and said, "You too."

A firefight ensued. One group of students escaped from a bus and began throwing rocks at a police car. Other students got the convey of buses back en route. Police fired on it. Students hit the floor but told their drivers to keep going. Bullets shattered bus windows. Investigators later found thirty bullet holes in one of the buses. The cops killed several people that night, including one student whose body was uncovered several days later. Accounts of his final moments differ: an autopsy showed that his eyes had been gouged out, facial tissue and muscle had been ripped off, his skull had been fractured, and several of his internal organs ruptured. You can take your pick of the gory details. But regardless what you choose, this showed "the level of atrocities committed that night," according to one investigator. Shortly after midnight of the day following the clashes with the police, three hooded men jumped out of an SUV and another vehicle and opened fire on an impromptu press conference taking place at the scene of the clash. They killed two students and injured several others.

Police rounded up surviving students and threw them in the slammer. A local gang called the United Warriors somehow took charge of the students. Details of the transfer were murky. The United Warriors believed that at least some of the students had ties to a rival gang called the Reds, who posed a threat to United Warriors' control of the region. On the strength of that belief, the Warriors executed all of the students and incinerated their bodies. The fire that consumed the corpses burned into the wee hours of the morning. Gang members then dumped the students' remains into plastic bags and threw them into the San Juan River. "We turned them into dust and threw their remains in the water," one of the murderers texted the gang leader. "They will never be found." A reporter for *La Jornada* telephoned the mayor of Iguala to find out what happened. The mayor told him, "Nothing happened."

More than one month after the students' abduction, the Mexican attorney general announced that several sacks filled with human remains had been found by a river close to the site where the students' bodies had been burned. An independent tribunal later issued two reports on the students' murder, accusing the Mexican government of stonewalling their investigation.

For its part, the TPP cited the massacre in Iguala in its final report:

> For all its painful impact and the documented connivance of the public authorities and the involvement of their agents, what happened at Ayotzinapa is merely another chapter in the long list of violations of the rights to dignity and life of the people of Mexico. They are a dramatic, real and symbolic expression of the relevance and meaning of the TPP's proposals.

Students have taken the brunt of official and corporate wrath in past episodes of Mexican history. An infamous 1968 massacre of students in the part of Mexico City known as Tlatelolco is one example. This was the incident that radicalized the young Comandante Marcos. Subsequently he became active in a Maoist group called National Liberation Forces. Students at Ayotzinapa had plans to ask for financial support to go to Mexico City for a march to mark the anniversary of the Tlatelolco massacre.

What happened in San Judas was on a smaller scale, but it was just as brutal as the massacres in Tlatelolco and Iguala. In 1980, the colonos of San Judas had constructed with their own hands a school named after the Mexican educator Alfredo Nava Sahagún. After Schmidt began his siege of the neighborhood, his henchmen dug trenches—six feet across, six feet deep—around the school to make the building almost impossible to access. The immediate vicinity of the two-classroom edifice looked like a World War I battlefield. Kindergarteners had no choice but to go through MS-13 checkpoints, where the guards ridiculed the kids.

One fateful morning in the fall of 2005, Maria Casango left her two younger children in her house when she took her older daughter Charlotte to school. She had given both of the younger children their breakfast and told her son Magdaleno, age four, "I'm leaving now, *papacito*. Look after your sister."

Magdaleno's sister Maria was three years old.

Mama Casango was on her way back home when her cousin Abigail came running toward her. There was a fire, she said. Maria could see the smoke, then the flame. At first it looked as if the garbage had taken on fire, but then she realized that, no, it was a house. It was her house.

"You could hear everything crackling inside," she said later.

She ran screaming toward the burning house. Abigail Casango and neighbors dragged her back. It was too late. Little Maria was found still in her bed. The body of her brother Magdaleno lay face up, with his back arched and his arms outstretched. He had made it to the tiny hall separating the children's room from their parents'.

Maria Casango began to scream. Neighbors had to carry her to Abigail's house.

"Why me?" she cried. "Why my children? Why couldn't I have died with them?"

The neighbors could commiserate. Like the Chorus in Euripides' play *Medea*, they could cry: "Ah! Poor lady, wither wilt thou turn?" Without water, it had been impossible to fight the fire. The police arrived late. The firefighters never came at all.

Officials reacted with caution to the incident: "We do not want the death of two minors politicized."

What the neighbors told Maria was that a couple of young cholos had been seen near the house carrying a plastic gallon jug and spilling a clear liquid from it. Had their boss ordered them to set fire to a house? In any event, they had gotten the wrong house.

The official verdict was that a short circuit was the cause of the fire. The chief of the fire department explained that "improvised electrical installations create a permanent risk of these kinds of tragedies occurring."

Maria's and Magdaleno's house had no electricity. Neither did their neighbors. All electricity to San Judas had been cut off months before.

MOVING TARGETS

Early in the twenty-first century, Mexico became a dangerous country for reporters. It was not always that way, but
things changed. Now Mexico was killing more journalists than Iraq. Little was said or written about it. When a
reporter in the state of Guerrero, in the south of the country,
was shot in the head, only one national paper, *La Jornada*,
covered the story. The local newspapers wrote nothing at
all about the murder.

When another reporter, Valentin Valdés Espinosa,
employed by *Zócalo de Saltillo*, was killed, a handwritten note
left beside his body explained, "This is going to happen to all
those who do not comply." His murderers had dumped the
body of the twenty-nine-year-old reporter in front of a motel.
Ropes pinioned his arms and legs. His body showed signs of
torture. He had been shot not once but over and over again.

"We are not going to get mixed up in this," said Vadés's editor. "I don't believe there will be results, so why push?"

An hour-long shootout in Ciudad Juárez passed without comment in the press.

El Diario published an editorial saying that it was willing to shape its news coverage to suit the demands of the cartels. It took this extraordinary step in order not to jeopardize its reporters' lives. "When a cartel comes here to ask us not to publish something, they're very diplomatic. They're not violent," said Pedro Torres Estrada, the editor of the newspaper. "When you have the power, though, you can be this way."

Cartels took to hacking email accounts of journalists to find out who their sources were and to track the whereabouts of the reporters themselves. Thugs broke into newsrooms, vandalized equipment, and stole computers. Newspapers routinely omitted reporter bylines and photographer picture credits from crime stories considered sensitive.

No one blamed Mexican journalists for taking self-protective action (or inaction). The intimidation was over-whelming. Eighty-eight journalists were killed in the first fifteen years of the twenty-first century. At the height of the violence against journalists, every ten days saw the murder of a Mexican journalist. One human rights organization reported that 89 percent of the murders of journalists went unpunished.

The killing came home to *El Diario* on a November morning in 2008. Armando Rodríguez was the newspaper's star reporter. He was a bluff, aggressive man. His nickname— Choco—came from a Mexican sweet that has a cream center and a chocolate covering. His colleagues thought that this pastry reflected Rodríguez's temperament.

The journalist's contacts inside the police and the judiciary were legendary. "Armando had better contacts than anyone with the police," said the executive editor of the newspaper. Fellow reporters used to say that he held unchallenged sway at police headquarters. His jokes were surefire. He could reduce a desk clerk to spasms of laughter one moment, then squeeze an interview out of a police commander the next.

Rodríguez played by his own rules. He brooked interference from no one. One day he had walked into his new editor's office, closed the door behind him, and told her, "I have a problem with authority."

Armando was the proverbial bull in a china closet. In his case, the china closet was a sprawling, untidy agglomeration called Ciudad Juárez. He was famous for playing the music he liked, and he played it loud and strong. To hell with what the neighbors thought. He was prolific, too, churning out on average four stories a day for the paper.

One morning in November 2008, Rodríguez was sitting in his car with his eight-year-old daughter. Armando used to drive her to school before beginning his workday at the newspaper. It was cold that morning, and the two of them tried to get warm by huddling over the warm air vent in the dashboard. They never saw the man who walked up to the car from behind and opened fire with a 9mm pistol, first through the driver's window, then through the windshield. There were six bullet holes, three in the driver's window, three in the windshield. Police later found a total of ten bullet casings around Rodríguez's car. The hit man—who was never apprehended—made his getaway in a waiting car.

Armando's wife Blanca was inside the house getting the couple's two-year-old daughter ready for daycare. She heard the shots. "Another shooting," she said to herself. Blanca peered through a curtain and saw her husband sitting upright behind the driver's wheel. He looked as if he was in the process of phoning *El Diario* to report the latest shooting. The Rodríguez's daughter sat beside him sobbing hysterically. Blanca ran outside and pulled her daughter from the car.

Back inside the house, she called for an ambulance. None ever came.

★

The violence in Ciudad Juárez took its toll on the way the city functioned. Businesses throughout town closed and merchants fled to El Paso. The restaurant operated by Las Hormigas, the one that Alfred Von Bachmayr and his helpers had insulated, had to close, although Lina Sarlat promised to reopen it as soon as the situation calmed down.

Settlers at San Judas had taken their case to the Agrarian Tribunal of Chihuahua. There several reporters received subpoenas to appear and testify. This was something they were understandably reluctant to do. Manuel del Castillo, the president of the Association of Ciudad Juárez Journalists, went along to show his solidarity with them. "Our profession is considered a high-risk one," del Castillo said. "Although we are not in a war zone, the presence of organized crime and the high level of corruption makes us vulnerable."

Journalists were not the only target of assassins. A lawyer representing the residents of San Judas was shot and killed as he sat in his truck outside the Agrarian Court in Chihuahua City. His murderers peppered his head with an AK-47. A total of nineteen bullets pierced the lawyer's brain.

When he heard of the assassination, Father Joe told the press: "They let his body lie in the street as a message. By the time the police got there, passersby were collecting shells as souvenirs." Then he said quietly, after a moment of reflection: "Even in death, you become a curiosity."

The Mexican press did not cover the lawyer's death widely. After all, it was only one of ten that day in the province of Chihuahua.

The colonos followed Subcomandante Marcos's advice and engaged a lawyer from Mexico City, Barbara Zamora, to represent them at the Agrarian Court.

"Life isn't about waiting for the storm to pass," Barbara Zamora had written on her Facebook page. "It's about learning to dance in the rain."

Barbara Zamora had a long and illustrious career as a defender of the most vulnerable groups in Mexican society. The name of her firm, Land and Liberty (Tierra y Libertad), was a slogan adopted by the EZLN. It was first used by a revolutionary group active in Russia toward the end of the nineteenth century. In recognition of her work, Zamora received the Ludovic Trarieux Award in 2003. This award was named after a French jurist active at the time of the Dreyfus Affair. Nelson Mandela was its first recipient. Zamora shared the prize with another Mexican lawyer, Digna Ochoa, who was awarded the prize posthumously, after her assassination in the fall of 2001.

Ochoa was a tiny woman of great courage. She once snuck into a military hospital to talk to a man being held there. In her own words:

> When I got to this room where this person was, the nurse at the door told me I could not go in. "We are not even allowed in," she said. I told her that I would take care of it myself. All I asked of her was that she take note of what I was going to do and that if they did something to me, she should call a certain number. . . . I took a deep breath, opened the door violently and yelled at the federal judicial police officers inside. I told them that they had to leave immediately, because I was the person's lawyer and needed to speak with him. They didn't know how to react so they left. I had two minutes, but it was enough to explain who I was, that I had been in touch with his wife, and to get him to sign a paper proving he was in the hospital. . . . By

then the police came back, and with the fierceness
that usually characterizes their behavior. Their first
reaction was to try to grab me. They didn't expect me
to assume an attack position—the only karate position I know, from movies, I suppose. Of course, I don't
really know karate, but they definitely thought that I
was going to attack. Trembling inside, I said sternly
that if they laid a hand on me, they'd see what would
happen. And they drew back, saying, "You're threatening us." And I replied, "Take it any way you want."

At the time of her death, Ochoa was representing two
activists who had protested illegal logging in the Sierra
Tarahumara. This was the region in which Eloy Vallina's
family had long-standing business interests. The Lawyers'
Committee for Human Rights claimed that Digna Ochoa's
clients had been "targeted by local authorities because they
opposed wildcat logging; they were held and tortured over
several days until they 'confessed' to marijuana cultivation
and weapons charges." The men languished for two years
in prison despite court appeals. The men's release from
prison occurred days after their lawyer was killed in her own
Mexico City office.

Ochoa was a nun. And she was an Indian. She had
studied law because her father, a union organizer in Veracruz,
had said repeatedly that he and people like him needed
lawyers, and the lawyers out there cost too much. Her father
was arrested, tortured, and detained for more than a year
before disappearing. "Anger is energy," she said once. "It's
injustice that motivates us to do something, to take risks,
knowing that if we don't, things will remain the same."

Mexican authorities first claimed that Ochoa's death
was a suicide, but that was impossible to swallow. Her assassins had left a note beside her body warning other "sons-
of-a-bitch" human rights lawyers that what happened to

Ochoa could happen to them. What nailed the phony suicide hypothesis was a forensic detail: a bullet wound in Ochoa's head showed that the bullet that killed her had penetrated her brain from the left side of her head, angling downward as it sped to the right. Ochoa, who was right-handed, would have needed to be a contortionist to kill herself like that.

Zamora was born in Mexico City. She studied law at the National Autonomous University of Mexico, graduating in 1988. At the time she began to represent the inhabitants of San Judas, she had been practicing law independently for a quarter of a century. The plight of indigenous people has long interested her. Though not herself a member of a Zapatista organization, she contributed regularly to Zapatista publications. A photograph in her Mexico City office shows her with Subcomandante Marcos. It hangs beside a sketch of Emiliano Zapata.

In the Agrarian Court of Chihuahua, delay followed delay. This was the theater in which Pablo Schmidt and the San Judas settlers waged their legal war. In June 2008, the presiding judge accepted a motion put forth by Pablo Schmidt's lawyer to dismiss the suit brought against the family by the settlers for lack of proof. The settlers were required to respond immediately to this charge. Later that month the judge ruled that a summons to any of the Schmidt henchmen would need to be served to them in person, at their houses, and not by an edict. Zamora, representing the colonos challenged this ruling.

In July 2008, the court asked the assistance of the Juárez municipality, the Federal Electricity Commission, and the Office of Public Security to locate the Mara Salvatrucha who were being summoned to testify at the court.

In August 2008, the Schmidt lawyers asked permission of the court to address the residents of San Judas directly to negotiate a settlement. Many of these residents were present in the court. Barbara Zamora turned to look them in the eye, to ask for their response to this offer of negotiation. They bellowed their response. It was an unequivocal "No!" Barbara Zamora demanded that the court act on the settlers' request for protection against the Schmidt family's threats and continuing harassment. When she attempted to present evidence of the settlers' claims, the presiding judge told her that the time to make such a submission had passed. (This decision was later reversed.)

In October 2008, the Agrarian Court admitted that a "small error" had been made in issuing summons for the MS-13: they had been published not in the state of Chihuahua but in the state of Zacatecas. More delays.

Later that month the court agreed to consider the colonos' complaints against the Schmidts at the beginning of the new year. Barbara Zamora issued a formal reprimand of the judge for his delaying to act on a plea that she had first made on behalf of the settlers five months earlier.

On January 8, 2009, the court postponed a New Year hearing because the Schmidt representative came without a lawyer. The next session of the Agrarian Court was scheduled for January 21. On that day, the Schmidts' legal representative presented the court with a medical document attesting to Pablo Schmidt's illness. The developer had contracted salmonella poisoning. The presiding magistrate accepted the document and deferred the next session of the court to February 3.

On January 30, 2009, the Agrarian Court announced that its docket was overloaded and the session scheduled for February 3 would be moved back to February 13. On February 13, the Schmidts' lawyer asked for a postponement of the session to give him time to understand the case against his client. The court agreed to postpone the session to February 24. February 24 came and went. The session that day was deferred. So was the session scheduled for March 10. As was April 4 session. June 16: this time Barbara Zamora was sick and could not attend a court session. The session was pushed back to August 4. So on and so forth.

How would the Zapatistas have reacted to this unending trickle of delays?

Ya basta!

TRUE RELIGION

The words "liberation theology" never passed his lips. Not during the time that Father Joe spent ministering to the needs of his parishioners in San Judas. This was a hot-button subject, developed by Catholic prelates in Latin America during the 1970s—theologians like Leonardo Boff and Gustavo Gutiérrez, who attempted to interpret Catholic beliefs in terms of Marxist categories.

As a child, Gutiérrez contracted polio. He spent the bulk of his Peruvian adolescence in bed. That experience predisposed him to contemplate a career in medicine. But midstream in his studies to become a doctor, he changed course and opted to become a priest. He studied in Europe, first at Leuven, the oldest university in Belgium, before going on to get a PhD from the French Université Catholique de Lyon. On his return to Lima, Gutiérrez worked as a parish priest in a Lima slum. There he came to realize that his education had not enabled him to deal effectively with the problems of his poor and persecuted parishioners. Poverty was not a virtue. That was one thing he quickly learned. Poverty was a destructive state, to be opposed relentlessly. At the time, he said:

> I live in a country in which about 60 percent of the population finds itself in a situation of poverty and 35 percent live in extreme poverty. A country where 120 out of every 1000 children die before reaching five years of age; a country where 2 of every 1000 people suffer from tuberculosis.

Leonardo Boff was a Brazilian theologian, born in December 1938. Like Gutiérrez, he studied in Europe and published his thesis, which he wrote at the University of Munich in German, as *Die Kirche als Sakrament im Horizont der Welterfahrung* (literally "The Church as a Sacrament in the Horizon of the World Experience"), one of his books for which there is no English translation. He criticized both the Church for being "fundamentalist" and secular power for fostering neoliberalism. This was something else that he characterized as fundamentalist. Boff wrote in *The Marriage of Heaven and Earth*:

> Today we are in a new phase of humanity. We all are returning to our common house, the Earth: The people, the societies, the cultures and religions. Exchanging experiences and values, we enrich ourselves and we complete ourselves mutually.

The starting premise of these men was that theology, rather than being a static collection of truths independent of time or place, should be based on scripture viewed "from below." Christians should see it from the vantage point of the poor and oppressed. Theology was a dynamic study that incorporated contemporary insights from disciplines like sociology and history.

In fact, theology began—in the view of priests like the Franciscan Gutiérrez—with action on behalf of the under-privileged of the world. First came action, which by necessity is revolutionary, and from it arose a theology: the theology of liberation. The liberation theologian plunges into the battle to transform society, to make the world a more equitable and just place in which the oppressed will be liberated and the poor freed from the weight of capitalism.

One liberation theologian defined sin as "unjust social structure." Sounding rather like Protestants, some lib-erationists held in contempt prayers to patron saints and the veneration of Mary, the mother of Jesus. (This actu-ally worked to their disadvantage among conservative and pious peasants in Latin America.) They ridiculed those in the Church who placed more importance on getting people to heaven than getting them decent living conditions.

Reaction inside the Catholic Church to liberation theol-ogy was mixed. In his encyclical *Evangelii Nuntiandi*, Pope Paul VI commented with sympathy and at length on the yearning of oppressed people for liberation. The movement has also received support from men like Bishop Samuel Ruiz of San Cristóbal in Mexico. While he might not condone the violence of the Zapatista movement, the bishop could identify with the way Zapatistas acted to free the indigenous people of Chiapas of everything that oppressed them.

His views, however, were not unanimously shared inside the Church. One Latin American bishop wrote, "When I see a church with a machine gun, I cannot see the crucified Christ in that church. We can never use hate as a system of change."

Despite his commitment to social justice, Pope John Paul II kept warning priests about becoming too involved in secular matters. "The conception of Christ as a political figure, as a revolutionary, as the subversive of Nazareth does not tally with the Church's catechism," he said.

And, of course, there was the nagging worry about the Marxist underpinnings of the new theology. The Vatican watchdog on doctrinal correctness took the view that it was impossible to embrace Marxist principles without adopting Marxist methods and goals, so Catholics should shun Marxism, pure and simple. For Boff, this was no problem:

> In liberation theology, Marxism is never treated as a subject on its own but always from and in relation to the poor. Placing themselves firmly on the side of the poor, liberation theologians ask Marx: "What can you tell us about the situation of poverty and ways of overcoming it?" Here Marxists are submitted to the judgment of the poor and their cause, and not the other way around.

> Therefore, liberation theology used Marxism purely as an instrument. It does not venerate it as it venerates the gospel. To put it in more specific terms, liberation theology freely borrows from Marxism certain "methodological pointers" that have proved fruitful in understanding the world of the oppressed.

In the mid-1980s one of Leonardo Boff's books, *Church: Charism and Power*, brought him into conflict with Vatican authorities. They judged Boff to have endangered the doctrine of the faith. It was only a matter of time before the Brazilian Franciscan got into seriously hot water. This was the man, after all, who had coauthored, with his brother Clodovis, an essay entitled *A Concise History of Liberation Theology*, in which he stated, "The poverty of Third World countries was the price to be paid for the First World to be able to enjoy the fruits of overabundance." Elsewhere, Leonardo Boff wrote "A questioning Christian cannot avoid feeling anguish. Has this pontificate [John Paul II's] taken us to the essence of Jesus' legacy?"

The straw that broke the camel's back came late in the decade in an essay that Boff wrote for a Catholic journal of which he was an editor. In 1991, Boff's superiors in the Franciscan Order stripped him of his editorship and ordered him to stop publishing his views for one year. No less than the president of Latin American bishops supported his censure. To no one's surprise, Boff quit the priesthood.

John Paul's successor as pope, Cardinal Ratzinger—who chose as his pontifical name Benedict XVI—branded liberation theology as a heresy and a threat to the church. At one time Ratzinger had been regarded as something of a liberal in the Church. But this was one leopard who could and did change his spots once he got tied up in Vatican politics as prefect of the Congregation for the Doctrine of the Faith. In 1984, he issued a treatise entitled "Instruction on Certain Aspects of the 'Theology of Liberation,'" which lambasted the liberationists. One of these liberationists, Juan Segundo, labeled the treatise "a general attack on Enlightenment humanism . . . aimed at re-establishing an otherworldly and transcendentalist religion."

Father Joe had enough on his plate without locking horns with Church heavyweights on theological issues. So he said nothing about liberation theology. Still . . . how could a priest like him—battling for his flock in places like the Agrarian Court of Chihuahua, literally standing between his parishioners and Pablo Schmidt's cholos in their physical clashes, writing about his people's struggles, organizing meetings and support groups and prayer vigils and bake sales on their behalf—how could he be immune to the lure of a philosophy that he, in practice, subscribed to? True, he dealt with a local problem, something that liberationists disdained. They favored sweeping gestures that had what they called a transformational quality. But recording what

Father Joe fought for impregnated his actions with the power for transformation. The good priest of San Judas was liberation theology in the flesh, in the blood, in the bone, a man who practiced what the liberationists preached.

Like Leonardo Boff, Father Joe had to be stopped. Boff was gagged. Joe Borelli was deported. One day in the fall of 2006, he was invited to the Ciudad Juárez office of the Mexican immigration authorities. The authorities told him that he was working illegally in Mexico. Technically this was true: he was working without a work permit. This was a requirement that was normally waived for clergy like Father Joe, but not in his case. Of course, he could always apply for a work permit, but this would have to be done outside the country. In El Paso, for example. In the meantime, he had to leave the country. "When one works for justice, this often doesn't please governments. It doesn't please the rich. And this has consequences," Father Joe said afterward.

Police escorted him to the Stanton Street Bridge where he crossed over into the U.S. As was previously mentioned, this was the first and only instance of a Catholic priest being deported from Mexico for working without a work permit. While he could apply for a work permit from El Paso, he was advised quietly, in an informal aside, and very politely—the way cartel bosses talk to newspaper editors—not to try.

Juárez bishop Renato Ascencio Leon said that he knew the good father had been deported but he had no other information. "Father Borelli is a non-Mexican," he said. You could taste the vinegar in his voice, "and he must abide by the immigration laws of the country." The bishop, one should note, was a member of the Vatican Council on Emigrants and Itinerants.

Joseph Borelli did not go far. He settled in at a Spiritan Order house in El Paso, less than one mile from the border. From there, he kept tabs on the situation in San Judas. But he was still not *there*, at a critical distance from the action.

That tamped down his contact with the people who had been his parishioners.

Attempts to wear down the settlers went on relentlessly. Early one January morning, a gang of thugs broke into the home of one of the colonos resisting relocation. The men had wrapped bandanas around their faces to conceal their identity. They began to loot the house of its belongings: furniture, an ancient fridge, even freshly watered plants. Dirty water splashed over the dirt floor of the house. What they could not filch, they destroyed with crowbars, pickaxes, and shovels, smashing windows and walls. Neighbors congregated at the site and started to yell at the thugs. Guadelupe Pineda, whose house was being torn apart, rushed out to stop a truck that was making off with her belongings. Her blouse caught on the railing of the truck. The driver accelerated. The woman was dragged along with the speeding vehicle. The driver leaned out his window and jeered at her struggles to free herself of the truck. Pineda's blouse was torn and the flesh of her breasts bruised before she could fall back away from the pickup truck.

The driver had the cheek to return to the scene of the incident with a couple of city cops. He claimed to have been accosted by residents of the neighborhood while he was cleaning up trash. The next day, when he went to file a complaint, police detained Pineda's husband and accused him of disturbing the peace. He was released only when civic groups pressed for action.

The two ex-nuns from Las Hormigas who had settled in San Judas tried to help the settlers, but there wasn't much that they could do. In any event, their special status in the community did not protect them from insult and harassment. The day they attempted to photograph the White Guards destroying property, one of the Mara Salvatrucha yelled to them to get the fuck away ("*Vayansen a la chinaga*"). The same man donned a goat's head mask and dashed toward the two women. He made grabbing gestures at Lina's skirt. Lina shrieked and flailed at her assailant. He managed to pull her skirt half way down her legs before backing off. He giggled at Lina's feeble defense.

When Father Joe heard of these outrages, he shook his head and quietly mumbled to himself, "Jesus Christ!" It was the only time people could remember his invoking the name of the Savior to express his disgust with the behavior of the Schmidt thugs.

Just after he was expelled from Mexico, Father Joe appeared before a meeting of the Doña Ana County Commission in New Mexico when it tabled a discussion of the situation in San Judas. What follows is an abridgement of the exchange that took place between the priest and the commissioners.

> *Commissioner One*: We have a human crisis in San Judas. In the process of developing the land that this neighborhood occupies, human rights have been violated. Two children have been burned alive in their home. Two adults have been killed. A gated community has been erected, with barbed wire and guard dogs, and men with baseball bats and guns that are outlawed in Mexico. Father Borelli, who is here with us today, was the minister of that community. His church was burned down. Now he is living in El Paso because his life has been threatened.
>
> *Father Joe*: I'm not here to say anything against development. I'm not a politician, but I am interested in justice and in human rights.
>
> We come to you because San Judas is in the middle of a huge multi-development project that involves a lot of federal, city, and state money and private developers. That piece of land on which San

Judas sits fronts New Mexico. So what happens there has an international dimension.

The chapel I took care of—Jesus de Nazareth— was located in San Judas. I knew nothing of any land dispute, and then, lo and behold, one day the electric infrastructure was ripped out of the community. From then on, there has been a program of low-intensity conflict designed to move people out of the area. There has been violence and intimidation. Through corruption and bribery, a community has been dismantled. That is the greatest sin of all.

Vigilantes came in and were there for three weeks. The police arrested them, but they came back. They set up a barbed-wire fence and a guard tower. The colonia was sealed off. Residents tried to tear down the fence, and there was a violent exchange between vigilantes, who were armed, and the residents, who were not. The police refused to intervene. The city refused to intervene.

The last time a human rights group came to San Judas, it was greeted by vigilantes with sticks and chains and guard dogs. The vigilantes refused to let the group pass the gate to San Judas. The chapel, Jesus de Nazareth, was knocked down by the vigilantes. But we rebuilt it in three days, bigger and better.

Commissioner Two: Yeah, Father. I've been looking into this matter for three or four months, and I've been talking to Senator Bingaman's people. What I'm hearing is that they are frustrated with the Mexican government. Bingaman is getting nowhere on this issue. We all want Governor Richardson to do something. What can be done to influence the governor of Chihuahua? How can we deal with this issue as we try to move forward as a region?

Father Joe: The head of the Federal Human Rights Commission in Mexico has been refused entry into San Judas. He recommended to the president of Mexico that the federal government intervene. His request met with total silence. The problem on the Mexican side is that there are too many links between people of power, people of wealth, and government officials.

What I can imagine coming from the U.S. side is a human pressure that we can exert. We can say, in effect, "If I'm going to do business with you, if we are going to negotiate a deal in which we both have something to gain, then we need to understand that this problem can throw a monkey wrench into the works. Development can't go forward if there is a perception that land is being acquired through violence, through intimidation."

Finally, if there is a public airing of what is happening, that will restrain the ones who are inflicting harm on the residents of San Judas. That, at least, is our hope, that the people who are still there will be treated with respect, that there will be a just and peaceful way to manage the land dispute.

Commissioner Two: I understand that, Father. It seems to me that the Mexican government should be stepping up to the plate here. My question is: Is it just the influence of the Mexican developers? Is it too much or what?

Father Joe: It's very strong. There's a lot of interaction between the developers on both sides of the border, between the governor. . .

Commissioner Two: How so, sir? You see, this is something I'm getting a little upset about. I've spent three to four months. . . There have been accusations that developers in El Paso are mixed up in this. But I've not found one set organizational connection there. There have been some allegations that Eloy Vallina—he's on the board of the Verde Group—that he's involved with these guys. I've been asking a lot of people, "Can someone define one set organizational relationship?"

Father Joe: I'm just saying you have very wealthy, very powerful people who obviously are meeting together. . . . The people in Grupo Verde know one another. They can talk to one another and try to exert their influence for the good. We wouldn't want anyone to think that we turned our backs on this injustice, allowed it to happen.

Border plans are stuff people from both sides of the frontier are talking about. How can we improve the infrastructure? How can we improve border access? So I'm asking, in that context, where business people are sitting down and talking to each other, can we exert pressure to get the gates out of there, to get the guards out of there? I'm not making any accusations.

Commissioner Two: I understand, sir. I just want to be very clear when we're talking about this issue that I wouldn't like to be . . . so and so is rich and powerful so they have something to do with this. I don't think that's fair.

Father Joe: I'm not saying that any more than I'm saying that Governor Richardson is causing it. But Governor Richardson can call the governor of Chihuahua on the phone and say, "Hey, compa, like what can we do about this?"

Commissioner Three: I think it would be naive to think that, on this side of the border, we have the ability to track these business relationships. I'll be polite and call it international business. It's structured in such a way that you cannot track it. Relationships are not transparent. I lived in Central and South America for many years and know that the rules are different. Government works in a certain way. Business works in a different way.

Commissioner Four: None of us can condone this sort of situation. And as a representative of this district, I'm appalled. I really am appalled. I just don't have the words to express how appalled I am. And I want to go see the area. That's home to me. Sunland Park is home to me. I will do everything in my power, if it means talking to Governor Richardson and the governor of Chihuahua, talking about intervening and stopping this violence and this injustice.

[*Applause from the audience*]

Commissioner Three: I think it would be remiss of us to walk away today with just a statement of outrage. This commission really needs to take an action. Let's do it. Let's not just sit and express our outrage. Let's go down there. Very quickly. Let's coordinate the people who have the knowledge and who have done the research and who are already involved in the issue. We need to keep the momentum going. This can't wait until two meetings from now when we can pass a resolution. This can't wait until we're able to tour the area and see what's going on. There are people out there without electricity, without heat, without water and sewers. This is a health violation. It's a human rights violation. And it's something that cannot continue at all. We need to issue a letter that is a call to action to show that Doña Ana County isn't going to sit on the sidelines.

[*More applause from the audience*]

★

The measure passed by the commission, wreathed in a garland of "whereas" clauses, advocated a "peaceful and just" resolution to the situation in San Judas. This included the restoration of electric power and a source of potable water in the disputed neighborhood and an examination by U.S. officials of the international aid resources available to assist in providing basic services to the residents of San Judas while "the situation is being resolved."

The one speaker to be called before the commission in the open comment session that preceded the vote was a lawyer representing Pablo Schmidt. He extended an invitation to the commissioners to visit San Judas to see for themselves that the situation "was not as serious as it was portrayed." He went on to say that he would personally recommend that Mexico City recognize New Mexico as Mexico's favorite state—*el estado mas favorecido de Mexico*—because of the support offered by Governor Richardson.

A reporter who covered the commission's proceedings asked to talk in confidence with Father Joe after the dust had settled on the commission's deliberations. Their meeting took place in a bar frequented by Las Cruces call girls. A wall-mounted TV was blasting out hip-hop lyrics as the men drank beer and yelled back and forth to each other in order to be heard. First off, the reporter told Father Joe that it was unusual—rare indeed—for the commission to limit the open session to one speaker. There had been a lot of arm twisting by New Mexico state officials in the governor's office, he said. They had warned the commission not to call for removal of the barbed-wire fence, not to call for respecting human rights, not to do anything that would jeopardize binational development in the region.

★

A forum at the University of Texas El Paso later that fall gave several residents of San Judas the opportunity to air their complaints in a dignified academic setting. The first to speak was a man named Aurelio Carranza, who told his audience of professors and students that he originally came from Zacatecas. He went on to say:

> I've lived in San Judas for more than thirty-five years. My parents passed on the property to me so that I could work the land. But now the Schmidt family has men come to beat us. They beat my wife. We're both elderly. We're living a horrible life. The vigilantes carry weapons, even high-powered rifles. Sometimes we get back home late at night and the gate is locked. If we tell the guards to open it, they get angry and beat us. There is nothing we can do about it.

Rafael Piñon also spoke at the forum. He told the audience that he had witnessed the deaths of Carmen Casango's children:

> I was there. I tried to open the door. It's very hard to talk about this. But the most painful thing was when we found one child in her bed and the other beside the door. One was four. The other was three. Their skin was charred. It was falling off their little bones. Forgive me. I don't know how to talk. But I have seen many things. Many things have taken place. But I'm not educated enough to explain them to you. I would want someone to tell you everything that happened.

The highlight of the forum was a panel consisting of two women, one—Petra Medrano—from San Judas, and the other—Lupe Ochoa—from the Segundo Barrio in El Paso. Both women had lived in their respective neighborhoods for fifteen years. They came to share their common struggle against developers from both sides of the border.

Medrano was dressed like a Mexican businesswoman, in a dark suit and a white blouse with short, horizontal stripes. Her dark brown hair was tied back in a ponytail. "We lived in peace there," she said. "We feel so powerless. I know that I'm a target now, but I must speak out."

"Why now?" she asked. "Why have they decided to kick us out now after we've been there for so long?"

Lupe Ochoa echoed Medrano's sentiments:

We used to live happily in our barrio, but now the Paso del Norte group has us living in fear. Residents have been selling their houses for fear that they will be forced out.

What connects us with San Judas is our love for our neighborhoods. Love is what unites us. The people who are doing this to us are not invincible. With all their money, they don't have the heart that we, the poor, have.

"It's the same people who are responsible for what is happening in San Judas," said Petra Medrano. "It's the same businessmen who are threatening us."

A couple of short documentary videos were shown, one about each community. In each of them, residents expressed almost identical sentiments about the seizure of their property. The videos linked development plans by Pablo Schmidt, Eloy Vallina, and Bill Sanders targeting the northwestern sector of Ciudad Juárez to the detriment of the people living there.

Father Joe commented that the project, which spanned San Judas, Sunland Park, San Jeronimo, and Santa Teresa, involves billions of dollars. "That's the price tag on the whole enchilada," he said.

The Doña Ana commissioners who had wanted to visit San Judas did not wait long to take up their invitation to come see for themselves what was going on. They arrived one afternoon, unannounced, and told the MS-13 guards that the Schmidt family lawyer had invited them. The guards contacted the man who took more than an hour to show up.

In the meantime, the commissioners were kept waiting at the neighborhood gate. When he arrived, the lawyer apologized for taking so long. He was wearing a flaming red tie. His suit looked as if he had bought it in Savile Row. His hair was slicked back over his ears.

"Why the barbed-wire fence," the commissioners asked. "To keep out intruders," the lawyer replied. This was a violation of the residents' rights. The lawyer smiled and said that this was private property.

The commissioners concluded that the situation was even worse than they had imagined. "I can't understand how this is happening in my own backyard," said one of them, a petite woman dressed in a pants suit and a narrow-brimmed hat, a shade of red decidedly more subdued than the lawyer's tie. "I see it, but I can't believe it."

"Something very wrong is going on here," said one of her male colleagues. "It's like a concentration camp."

"You can be sure that Governor Richardson is going to hear about what's happening here," said the commissioner in the red velvet hat.

The lawyer smiled again. He waved goodbye as the commissioners took their leave of San Judas.

The commissioners' experience was not unique. A human rights forum on-site was planned for the fall of 2007. It came off although not as planned. As soon as outside participants arrived, the Schmidt cholos swarmed the gate to San Judas, waving sticks and pipes and screaming insults at the newcomers. Two of the cholos came on horseback. One of the thugs grabbed a dog by the scruff of his neck. Guffawing and prancing back and forth on his horse, he thrust the cur's cock at the visitors from Las Cruces and wagged it at them. One of the female organizers of the forum said:

> It was a terrifying experience. I found it strange
> that there were women with the guards. They were

tough-looking, female versions of the male gang members. They seemed to be hiding in the guard-room beside the gate. I guess that if the guards decided to assault the women in the forum, it would look better if other women came to beat us up rather than the men.

Again the police were present. Again they refused to intervene. They were there to ensure that there were no alter-cations, they said. That was all.

Willivaldo Delgadillo, an activist who attended the forum, commented that "Juárez is world-famous for its murdered women, but now it's going to become famous for its concentration camp at San Judas." Delgadillo said of the forum:

> We were not allowed to go in, and the residents were not allowed to come out, so we set up the forum at the fence, one group of people inside the barbed wire and the other group outside.

"Our city is being divided up by powerful developers," he added. "The question from now on is going to be 'What side of the fence are you on?'"

A local historian, David Romo, wrote that some property values in the area had increased twenty-six-fold. Unsolicited buyers had come by, offering close to $40 thousand for a sliver of a sand dune. "I don't know what to do or think," he quoted one man as saying. "It seems strange to me that they are offering so much money just for a small property."

Undeterred by the fracas generated by the first San Judas forum, well-intentioned Las Cruces activists tried a second time. This time, the participants from New Mexico did not make it to the fence surrounding San Judas. Several of the MS-13 cholos, armed with baseball bats and accompa-nied by snarling dogs—one of them a pit bull held on a leash by the leader of the Schmidt goons—blocked the road about a quarter of a mile from the concentration camp.

"The people who live here have free access," said a Schmidt family rep. "But those who come to create conflict can't enter. We don't see any reason for them to be here." The activists from Las Cruces clustered a few feet away from the jeering guards. They had planned to set up a tent and a microphone for the participants in the forum: speakers, poets, and musicians. But Mara Salvatrucha thwarted their arrangements.

Once again the organizers of the forum asked the police to dismantle the barricade separating them from the gate leading into San Judas. Once again, the police demurred. Only their superior could order them to do that, they said, and he wasn't around. The forum attendees retreated to reconvene several feet farther down the road where they pitched their tent. There they stood, ankle-deep in sand, to denounce the injustice, the hatred, and the hostility to which they had come to bear witness.

Father Joe did not attend the disrupted forums at San Judas. How could he since he had been banished to El Paso by the Mexican immigration authorities? But no one could accuse him of laxness in the defense of his parishioners. His efforts on their behalf earned him no rebuke from his superiors in Pennsylvania, but he was careful about how he acted. Nothing he did was illegal—even in the narrowest sense of the word—and when he spoke, he eschewed language that could be viewed as anti-Catholic. The subject of liberation theology, for example, had never come up in his dealings with parishioners.

The suspicion generated in the Church by liberation theologians' use of Marxist terminology eased under Pope Francis, but contrary to what some people chose to believe about him, the pope who made gestures on behalf of the poor and who criticized the greed of the wealthy was not a liberal Protestant in a white skull cap. He held strong views about the sanctity of the priesthood, and he stopped short of endorsing revolutionary violence or any Marxist tenets.

"We pledge to work harder so that our Latin American and Caribbean Church may continue to accompany our poorest brothers on their journey even to martyrdom," he said. He later moved to accelerate the promotion of Bishop Oscar Romero of San Salvador—who was gunned down as he said mass in 1980—to the status of "blessed." This move had been stymied for years by Church reactionaries leery of Romero's leftist politics.

"Romero is a man of God," Francis said. "There are no doctrinal problems, and it is very important that the beatification be done quickly." (In fact it was done in Rome in 2018.)

The news rang as an angelic hymn in Father Joe's ears as he sat in his room at the Spiritan House in El Paso. The room, lighted solely by an old-fashioned desk lamp, was bereft of decoration. Only a crucifix hung above an iron frame bed. The crucifix, made of twisted rebar, tinfoil, and discarded lumber, had been a gift from a San Judas resident. As simple as it was, Father Joe's room was like an apartment in the Vatican in comparison to the shack that he had occupied in San Judas.

During his 2016 visit to Mexico, Pope Francis visited Chiapas. He prayed before the tomb of Bishop Samuel Ruiz in the Cathedral of San Cristóbal de las Casas. The bishop had died in 2011. The pope couldn't visit Chiapas without acknowledging the legacy of Samuel Ruiz. This, at least, was the opinion of Gaspar Morquecho, the journalist who had lost a night's sleep, so excited had he been at the Zapatistas' takeover of San Critóbal in 1994. "We're talking easily of a half century of social ministry work," said Morquecho, "and, starting in the '60s, having a preferential option for the poor." Among other acts of solidarity with the local community, Francis had reversed a ban on the ordination of indigenous deacons imposed after Ruiz retired.

At an open-air mass in the city's sports arena, attended by tens of thousands of people attired in brilliant Indian shawls and skirts, Pope Francis issued a ringing endorsement of indigenous rights.

"Some have considered your values, cultures, and traditions inferior," he intoned. "Others, dizzy with power, money, and the laws of the market, have stripped you of your lands and then contaminated them."

The pope paused for several long, long seconds before saying: "Sorry, brothers."

Local musicians played marimbas. The mass included readings in three native languages. And the pope's miter was emblazoned with a traditional Chiapas design.

Francis' appeal was a clear echo of liberation theology, and a call—like Leonardo Boff's—to build the Kingdom of Heaven on Earth. "The Pope came to tell us that the Mexican state should apologize, the way he did," one indigenous activist told the press. "It is an important action in a country where most Mexicans, as well as the political class and the majority of the Church, do not want to look at indigenous people."

Francis' action was an affirmation of Father Joe's own deeply ingrained opinions: the pope had enunciated the views of a humble priest who had worked tirelessly to protect his own impoverished flock on a windswept mesa of northern Mexico.

THE WRAP-UP

Manny wore a shirt with fading blue stripes. He was still a ruggedly handsome man. His pencil-thin mustache had blossomed into a luxuriant bush. He was unshaven. I had come to know him when he worked on insulating the restaurant funded by Las Hormigas. This was the project that Alfred von Bachmayr had directed. He looked older now, stockier and sadder. His days as the village gallant were clearly behind him, little more now than a half-forgotten memory. Manny's daughter Sophia, eight years old, with tangles of black hair framing her face and the eyes of an attentive doe, sat beside him. A motherless child, she was wearing a short sleeve flowered dress. She said nothing until the very end of the interview.

"They are one family, one son and his mother, and they have destroyed the lives of 250 families.

"There have been deaths here. You know that.

"The papers are saying that this highway of theirs was made for the Santa Theresa bridge. It cost 250 million pesos.

"They've put up a sign by the gate to San Judas. It says 'Private Property.' How can San Judas be private property if the land is in dispute?

"My father was one of the first settlers here. One day this land will be my daughter's. It was paid for in blood. It's ours and we must defend it."

"Do you want to leave?" he asks his daughter.

She shakes her head "no."

"We can get another house," he baits her.

"No," she says. "I grew up here."

"Her mom is no longer with us," Manny says. "There are only memories. That's all that's left."

To his daughter: "You're not afraid?"

"No."

"Why?"

"I'm used to it. And I have my Dad."

She buries her face in his shoulder.

Lucy Carrillo's patio was a patch of prettiness in the midst of a wasteland. It was filled with pots of red geraniums and purple-blue lavender. I could imagine being back in the southwest of France. The house was an austere structure of adobe and salvaged wood pallets. The corridor faced east. From there, you could see the traffic from the bridge at Santa Theresa that choked the highway. It was less than two miles away. Lucy's friends had helped her build an earthenware oven, because she liked to cook, and she was good at it. Here Lucy made her cheese-covered tortillas and crackling every weekend. Saturdays and Sundays were the days when her sons came to visit from the other side of the border.

On a day in mid-fall 2012, I had returned to San Judas to meet some of the colonos who had stuck it out there—and to eat Lucy's frijoles, nopales, and rice. Lucy's guests drank beer chilled with chunks of ice that she had gotten from God knows where. Her guests included Elvia Villalobos and Lina Sarlat. The two ex-nuns were always together. They were like Siamese twins. They never ventured out, it seemed, the one without the other. Maybe that was the enduring influence of their past lives in a convent. Manny was there as well as another of Von Bachmayr's crew, the once quiet and unassertive Mexican American, José Bernal, known to everyone as Ojos del Lobo. Evaristo and his wife Lara had also come back to the old neighborhood from their relocation site, where they were trying to make a fresh start with their little grocery store. They were active in a San Judas co-op that made pizza and salsa. They were searching for markets, both local and in the U.S., for their products. The co-op was considering branching out to produce more food items. "We've formed a co-op so we can get ahead and pay expenses," Lara explained. "Sometimes some of us don't work, since we have to be here taking care of a home or a piece of property."

From Lucy Carrillo's patio, we looked out over a flock of scrawny chickens and her few goats nibbling contentedly on kernels of corn that lay on the ground. I noted now what others had noted and commented on, how her eyes were soft and brown and silent as the Aztec ruins.

"I lived here, off and on, for thirty years of my life," José Bernal began in English before lapsing into Spanish.

Everyone grew silent as he spoke.

"I grew up here, like many of the people I know. And it is here where they wish to remain, where our parents built their houses, erected the school, made the streets, and hauled the water. Why the fuck should we leave this behind?"

José Bernal came up for air while the women in the group took care of the rest of us. They were anxious that there was enough red chili to keep our plates hot-spiced. The night, after all, was cooling down with a wind off the desert. José went on with his narrative:

If they wanted this land, why didn't they just talk to us? No, they threw us to their thugs. And their dogs. They insulted the women and scared the kids. Then they brought in their bulldozers and began pulling down the first houses. There was nothing we could do to stop them.

José concluded each paragraph, almost each sentence, with a hissing noise, a snakelike kind of laugh. Was he amused or outraged by what he had to say? It was hard to tell. Maybe something in between amusement and outrage, or a combination of the two.

Subcomandante Marcos had advised his audience in Chiapas to "cultivate a sense of humor, not only for your own mental and physical health, but because without a sense of humor you're not going to understand, and those who don't understand, judge, and those who judge, condemn."

One year before, José and other colonos had broken through police barricades to approach the man who was then President of Mexico. They demanded that he do something about the situation in San Judas. The president had promised to review the case. Later that year the Federal Executive ordered a high-ranking official in the Department of Agriculture to talk to the settlers. At the first of their meetings, they presented the official with documented proof of their right of possession. They showed him the decree of April 17, 1975, from the Department of Agriculture that stated that the twenty-five thousand hectares on which San Judas stood were federal property on which they were entitled to settle. They complained of the delaying tactics they had encountered at the Agrarian Reform Court. They proposed as an alternative to the court a "Dialogue Table" where not only they but representatives of the Schmidt family would meet face to face. At one of their last encounters with the government official, they laid out a statement signed by

U.S. activists, academics, and intellectuals urging a just and dignified resolution of the conflict. The government official offered to act as a mediator, but he did not offer any guarantees for a solution of the problem. The settlers understood. The one thing that they could do was to persevere—and resist.

"We were warriors and as such we knew our role and our moment." That is what Marcos said at the end of his career with the Zapatistas as Subcomandante Marcos. He had in mind a transformation, a migration of souls, a shift of personas. "SuperMarcos went from being a spokesperson to being a distraction," he said. "Those who loved and hated SuperMarcos now know that they have loved and hated a hologram. And we saw that now the hologram was no longer necessary."

> One day Marcos's eyes were blue, another day they were green, or brown, or hazel, or black—all depending on who did the interview and took the picture. He was the back-up player of professional soccer teams, an employee in department stores, a chauffeur, a philosopher, a filmmaker, and the et ceteras that can be found in the paid media. There was a Marcos for every occasion.
>
> At this very minute, in other corners of Mexico and the world, a man, a woman, a little girl, a little boy, an elderly man, an elderly woman—a memory— is beaten cruelly and with impunity, surrounded by the voracious crime that is the system, clubbed, cut, shot, finished off, dragged away among jeers, abandoned, their bodies then collected and mourned, their lives buried.

This was a speech Marcos delivered shortly after a comrade, a Zapatista teacher named José Luis Solis López, also known as Galeano, had been murdered. "We think," he offered, "that it is necessary for one of us to die so that

Galeano lives. To satisfy the impertinence that is death, in place of Galeano we put another name, so that Galeano lives and death takes not a life but just a name—a few letters empty of any meaning. That is why we have decided that Marcos today ceases to exist."

What had Marcos said about future generations?

> Those who were children in January 1994 are now young people who have grown up in the resistance. They have been trained in rebel dignity, lifted up by their elders throughout those twelve years of war. These young people have a political, technical, and cultural training that we who began the Zapatista movement did not have. These youth are now sustaining our troops more and more, as well as assuming leadership positions in the organization.

Whether Marcos was a hologram or not, whether his eyes were blue or green or brown, whether he was the back-up player of a professional soccer team or an employee in a department store, a chauffeur, a philosopher, or a filmmaker, whatever he was or would be, José had become a committed Zapatista.

"At last, someone who understood that we were not looking for shepherds to guide us, nor flocks to lead to the promised land," Marcos had said. "Neither masters nor slaves. Neither leaders nor leaderless masses. We realized that there was already a generation that could look at us face to face, that could listen to us and talk to us without seeking a guide or a leader, without intending to be submissive or becoming followers."

Back on the patio of Lucy Carrillo's house, José went on to tell us what he knew of the issues confronting the settlers:

> Listen, I'm a humble man, but I've been fortunate enough to get some education, and I believe that if

someone wants something that doesn't belong to him, then he has to ask for it. Shit, this family that is said to help poor people, a family that is on buddy-buddy terms with the bishop of Chihuahua, a family that does all these goody-goody things, this family tries to take San Judas by force. What do you make of that?

The settlers of San Judas are peaceful people. They went to the law to resolve this mix-up about the land. Remember, they've always worked the land. They built chicken coops. They had goats and cows and horses. But this is all gone now that the Schmidt family's guards have forced so many of them to abandon their land. This was their plan all along, to clear people off this site. They knew beforehand that the authorities were on their side.

At first they said that these lands were not ours. They belonged to their boss. We went to the police, but it was no use. Patrols of guards went through, time and time again, but the police did not intervene. There were rows, but the police did nothing. Back in March 2004, Mara Salvatrucha circled the neighborhood with barbed wire. A group of men stationed themselves beside the water tower outside San Judas, and they began to watch the settlers' movements. When men went down into the city to work, the cholos took advantage of their absence to wreck their houses, burn the *marraneras*, and chop down the trees.

At this point, Lina Sarlat took up the thread of the colonos' grievances. "From the beginning of this brawl, San Judas and its residents were subjected to a regime of annoyances. The worst of these were the barbed-wire encirclement of the neighborhood and our sense of isolation."

From a cardboard box, Lina drew a packet of papers and crumpled newspaper articles. She spread these out on a table before for us to look at. She smoothed out each article and read the title of each story to make sure that she had them in the right order. One of the articles dealt with the enormous gate that the MS-13 installed at the entrance to the neighborhood. There armed guards controlled the passage into San Judas. They began to search, item by item, what each of the residents of the neighborhood brought into San Judas. Lina said:

> They closed off all the streets. We thought that only the municipality had the right to open and close streets. But San Judas has become a law onto itself. It doesn't seem to matter that the Federal Electoral Institute has registered the nomenclature of our neighborhood. Although Pablo Schmidt claims that San Judas does not exist, there is evidence that contradicts that. See, here is Lucy Carrillo's voter registration card.

She handed around Lucy's papers. "You can see the name of the street and the house number where she lives."

At this point, the conversation turned to the neighborhood school. Lucy Carrillo's guests rose and walked to the building so that we could see for ourselves what had happened. The school was now abandoned. The door was missing. The windows had all been smashed. I could make out what was left of the ditch that the Schmidt cholos had dug around the building to control access to it. Guards had slept at the gate beside a rickety bridge that led across the ditch into the school.

"We have photos of children scampering across that ditch to get into the school," Lina said. "And we have testimonials from parents telling about the threats that the guards here made when children tried to cross the bridge."

Father Joe and his allies had put up a helluva fight to save that school, the Alfredo Nava Sahagún Primary School of San Judas. In the fall of 2011, volunteer teachers organized

classes for the children of San Judas in front of the offices
of the secretary of education in Ciudad Juárez. The children
shared a few plastic chairs and one plywood table or squat-
ted on the floor beside a big banner that read "Justice and
Liberty for San Judas." A couple of teachers made do with
one portable blackboard and a fistful of colored chalk. The
authorities were indifferent, even hostile, to the functioning
of the school in San Judas. They had stopped the delivery of
instructional materials to the school. The secretary of education for the province of Chihuahua had ordered an investigation of the situation in the neighborhood. It never happened.
After four months of their children's sit-in, the parents and
their supporters threw in the sponge. On a day in mid-
January 2012, after an all-day fast, the settlers discontinued
their protest. In a statement issued to the press, they pledged
to continue looking for "other forms of peaceful protest" and
to continue looking until they had secured justice.

"The sacrifice of those of us who have confronted the
hostility of economic power in San Judas is an education
that, sooner or later, will come to a good end," they wrote in
their statement. "It is a seed that will make the desert fertile."

Sup Marcos had said: "In order to rebel, neither mes-
siahs nor saviors are necessary. One only needs a sense of
shame, a bit of dignity, and a lot of organization."

The dinner at Lucy Carrillo's ended on a somber note.
Looking out from the terrace of her house, we could see little
apart from desert sprawl. Few of the original houses of the
neighborhood were still standing. They were as dark and
quiet as a long forgotten cemetery, silhouetted like lonely
sentries against the twilight sky.

The one building still intact and unscarred by the battle
for the land, the one that we could see from her patio, was
the clinic previously staffed by the Sisters of Charity. For
some reason, this had escaped destruction at the hands of
MS-13. But the nuns who used to work there had long since

departed. I remembered our single visit to the clinic years before. It had specialized in treating children with neurological disorders. These were unusually high in the border region between Mexico and the U.S., possibly because of working conditions in the maquilas. The Sisters of Charity would bathe children in a whirlpool tub. During our visit years before, we had watched a nun prepping a little girl for her bath. Her eyes were like luminous lumps of coal, glowing in her emaciated face. She had been dressed in a diaper and a rust-red sweater. She could not walk. Her legs were like muscleless spindles. To support her weight in the tub, there was a chain and a mesh net dangling from the end of a rod. An assortment of bathing suits, turned inside out, hung like laundry limply drying on the rod.

Apart from this one derelict clinic, there was little to see but the road that ran through San Judas, a road that had displaced so many families and caused so much grief and injury, had gotten Father Joe thrown out of the country, and had cost the lives of at least one adult and two children. José Bernal approached me. He looked me in the eyes. It was an aggressive stare, eyeball to eyeball. Los Ojos del Lobo. Very personal and impossible to evade. He asked simply, "So?"

I pondered that one syllable challenge. It was a challenge no writer with a commitment to social justice could ignore. Then I replied, "I'll think it over."

How could I write the story of San Judas? How could anyone do justice to what Father Joe and the colonos of the neighborhood had done and what they had endured? And all those, both in Mexico and in this country, present and past, who had sacrificed for the cause they believed in, for land and liberty? How could any writer offer an inkling of their devotion to that cause or pay adequate homage to their courage? One could start by quoting a line from the speech that La Pasionaria had given to the International Brigades on the eve of their departure from Spain at the end of the

Civil War of the 1930s: "*You can go proudly. You are history. You are legend. You are the heroic examples of democracy's solidarity . . . in the face of . . . those . . . with their eyes on hoards of wealth.*"

I did think about it. And I decided to write the story. Why? There is no answer to that question. Maybe simply so the saga of San Judas will not be forgotten. Nothing can be done to right the wrongs inflicted on the colonos of San Judas. But at least their story would be told.

Insulating the Hormigas' restaurant is where it had all begun, at least for me, as we stood on the porch of Casa Amistad looking out over San Judas, past the shell of an abandoned school bus, its wheels half-buried in sand. That's where it began, and this is where it now ends.

ACKNOWLEDGEMENTS AND ADMISSIONS

What does one say at the end of a book like this?

Woven into the fabric of the story are references to actual persons, to what they said and did and wrote. The organizations that appear in the second half of the book actually exist. I have adapted their reports to fit the fictional skeleton of my story. Apart from that adaptation, none of the quotes attributed to them have been made up.

San Judas—Saint Jude in English—is the patron saint of lost causes. Father Joe is my creation, but the character owes much to Bill Morton, the parish priest who lived in Anapra on the outskirts of Ciudad Juárez until his expulsion from Mexico by government authorities. The Schmidt family is my invention, all four generations of it. So is my chthonic demiurge José Bernal.

At one level, this book is about a land dispute in the north of Mexico. At another level, it deals with the impact of the North American Free Trade Agreement on Mexico and the United States. Canada is also a signatory to that agreement, but to have included it here would have led me too far afield. At bedrock, the book looks at the eternal struggle between good and evil, viewed from a uniquely Christian perspective.

This book would never have seen the light of day if it weren't for the guidance, the critical advice, and the suggestions offered by a host of friends. I am deeply indebted to them and to my sources. I shall list some of them, in no particular order, and indicate why I am grateful to them. Apologies to those I have inadvertently omitted.

First there is the intrepid Bill Morton. For years, he defended the residents of his neighborhood against the avarice of Mexican property developers. His courage in fighting these people was legendary. It is the stuff of which sainthood is made. I am indebted to him for having piqued my interest in the subject. I thank Barbara Zamora for taking so much time out of her busy schedule to talk to me about her role in the struggle for land and liberty. She and Bill Morton are among those to whom this book is dedicated.

My exposure to the subject of this book came about when I worked as a volunteer on a construction project in the barrio of Anapra. The leader of the project was the Santa Fe architect Alfred Von Bachmayr, who died in 2013. I have used our work as the basis for the first chapter of the book. Thank you, Von, for the opportunity to join your team. Rest in peace, good man.

Patrick Lynch gave generously of his time to answer my questions about Boston's North End and the Boston Latin School. He also read the manuscript of this book and made many helpful suggestions about ways to improve it.

Molly Malloy and Charles Bowden (1945–2014) were both supportive when I approached them for help. The State University of New Mexico made available to me the valuable thesis by Jon Williams. His advisor Neil Harvey had alerted me to the existence of this work. Dr. Harvey also took the time to talk to me, and for this I am grateful.

Father Daniel Welch of Duquesne University was very helpful in clarifying some points about the Congregation of the Holy Ghost. I am pleased to acknowledge his assistance.

Of course, I consulted a number of authors and journalists in preparing this book. I have listed these in the bibliography at the end of the book. Let me single out for special thanks Mary Jo McConahay. Her conscientious reading of the book was invaluable, and it was she who drew my attention to the Leonardo Boff quote.

Most of all, I need to acknowledge all of the work done by my collaborator Gavin Snider, whose sketches begin all but one chapter of the book. The cover is also Gavin's.

The errors in the book are mine, no one else's. I just hope that there are not too many.

I want to thank my editor Terry Bisson of PM Press for his patience and sympathy in working with me to bash this book into its present shape. Muchas gracias, Terry. Tu trabajo fue muy apreciado. My copy editor, Michael Ryan, did a smash bang-up job of whipping the text into readable shape, and I thank him for that.

Lastly, I dedicate the book to the freedom fighters in Mexico and the United States, some of whom lost their lives in the pursuit of truth, justice, and honor.

ABOUT THE AUTHOR

Robert Fraga is a mathematician by profession. Born in Massachusetts, he grew up in Los Alamos, New Mexico, where his father worked on the Manhattan Project during World War II. He himself worked as a summer student at the Los Alamos National Lab. He has taught both in the U.S. and abroad, principally in the Near East. He currently divides his time between Lawrence, Kansas, and the southwest of France, where he and his wife have restored a medieval/Renaissance house. They have two sons, one a computer entrepreneur in San Francisco, the other a pathologist at the University of Kansas. Both are married and have families of their own.

BIBLIOGRAPHY

"The AC Rating." *Navy Air Traffic Controller*, September 12, 2015. Accessed February 8, 2019. https://www.navycs.com/navy-jobs/air-traffic-controller.html.

Adams, David. "The Low Road to Hope in Juarez." *St. Petersburg Times*, May 30, 2005.

Agren, David. "Cristero Martyr Now a Popular Patron of Mexican Migrants Headed to US." *Catholic Free Press*, June 6, 2012. Accessed February 8, 2019. https://catholicfreepress.org/news/cristero-martyr-now-popular-patron-of-mexican-migrants-headed-to-us.

———. "In Mexico's Chiapas State, Bishop Ruiz Leaves Large Legacy." *National Catholic Reporter*, January 28, 2016. Accessed February 8, 2019. https://www.ncronline.org/news/world/mexicos-chiapas-state-bishop-ruiz-leaves-large-legacy.

Aguilar, Julián. "Twenty Years Later, Nafta Remains a Source of Tension." *New York Times*, December 7, 2012. Accessed Febraury 8, 2019. https://www.nytimes.com/2012/12/07/us/twenty-years-later-nafta-remains-a-source-of-tension.html?mtrref=www.google.com.

"Air Traffic Control A School." *NAVYdep.com*, May 20, 2013. Accessed February 8, 2019. http://www.navydep.com/forums/showthread.php?t=4143.

Aitkin, Gary. *Insulating a Concrete Block Building Using Pallets, Straw and Clay: World Hands Project*, 2008.

Amendáriz, Sergio. "Eloy Vallina." *El Diario*, December 2, 2013. Accessed February 11, 2019. http://diario.mx/Opinion/2013-12-01_f89b89a8/eloy-vallina/.

Bacon, David. "How U.S. Policies Fueled Mexico's Great Migration." *Nation*, January 23, 2012. Accessed February 8, 2019. https://www.thenation.com/article/how-us-policies-fueled-mexicos-great-migration/.

Baker, VL. "NAFTA Is Making Mexico Sick." *Daily Kos*, July 26, 2013. Accessed February 7, 2019. https://www.dailykos.com/stories/2013/7/26/1226585/-NAFTA-is-making-Mexico-sick.

Batstone, David. "Bishop Samuel Ruiz and the Zapatistas." *Aisling Magazine*, nd. Accessed February 7, 2019. http://www. aislingmagazine.com/aislingmagazine/articles/TAM19/Ruiz.html.

Bellinghausen Enviado, Hermann. "Corremos la frontera al otro lado en respuesta a la guerra de conquista de EU." *La Jornada*, November 3, 2006. Accessed February 8, 2019. https://www. jornada.com.mx/2006/11/03/index.php?section=politica&article =018n1pol.

Berg, Jeff. "Lomas de Poleo Lawyer Killed in Chihuahua City." *Newspaper Tree*, June 27, 2008.

Bloom, Greg. "Tarahumara Community Activists Jailed: Another Montiel-Cabrera Embarrassment for Mexico?" *La Presna San Diego*, May 16, 2003. Accessed February 7, 2019. http://www. laprensa-sandiego.org/archieve/may16-03/montiel.htm.

Boff, Leonardo, and Clodovis Boff. "A Concise History of Liberation Theology." In *Introducing Liberation Theology*. Maryknoll, NY: Orbis Books, 1987.

Boyer, Christopher R. *Political Landscapes: Forests, Conservation, and Community in Mexico*. Durham, NC: Duke University Press, 2015.

Briones, Pedro Sanchez. "Apoyan a Mujeres en Proyecto de Autoempleo; Construyen Local." *El Diario*, April 12, 2008.

Burnett, John. "Explosive Theory of Killings of Juarez Women." *National Public Radio*, April 23, 2015. Accessed February 8, 2019. https://www.npr.org/templates/story/story.php?storyId=1532607.

———. "Who's Killing the Women of Juarez?" *National Public Radio*, February 22, 2003. Accessed February 8, 2019. https://www.npr. org/templates/story/story.php?storyId=1171962.

Campbell, Monica. "Despite Violence, Journalists in Mexico Innovate to Report." *Nieman Reports*, October 20, 2015. Accessed February 8, 2019. https://niemanreports.org/articles/ despite-violence-journalists-in-mexico-innovate-to-report/.

Cana, Arturo. "Lomas del Poleo: lucha entre pobreza y avaricia." *La Jornada*, March 19, 2009. Accessed February 8, 2019. https://www. jornada.com.mx/2009/03/19/sociedad/048n1soc.

Carlsen, Laura. "NAFTA Is Starving Mexico." *Foreign Policy in Focus*, October 20, 2011. Accessed February 9, 2019. https://fpif.org/ nafta_is_starving_mexico/.

Chandler, Carmen Ramos. "CSUN Acquires Works by Mexican Photographer Julián Cardona." *CSUN Today*, January 16, 2013. Accessed February 8, 2019. http://csunshinetoday.csun.edu/arts-and-culture/ csun-acquires-works-by-mexican-photographer-julian-cardona/.

Chomsky, Noam. "Free Trade." In *Secrets, Lies, and Democracy*. Tucson, AZ: Odonian Press, 1994.

Comar, Scott. "A Historical Image of El Paso's Segundo Barrio," January 26, 2012. Accessed January 7, 2019. https://scottcomar. wordpress.com/2012/01/26/105/.

Commission of Solidarity and Defense of Human Rights A.C. and the Texas Center for Policy Studies. "The Forest Industry in the Sierra Madre of Chihuahua," July 2000. Accessed February 7, 2019. http://www.texascenter.org/publications/forestry.pdf.

Committee to Protect Journalists. "Luis Carlos Santiago." Accessed February 8, 2019. https://cpj.org/data/people/luis-carlos-santiago/.

Common Dreams Staff. "Study Links NAFTA to Obesity Epidemic in Mexico." *Common Dreams*, April 5, 2012. Accessed February 8, 2019. https://www.commondreams.org/news/2012/04/05/ study-links-nafta-obesity-epidemic-mexico.

Cope, Dorian. "The Zapatista Uprising." *On This Deity*, January 2, 2011. Accessed February 8, 2019. http://www.onthisdeity. com/1st-january-1994-%E2%80%93-the-zapatista-uprising-begins/.

Curtiss, Roger. "The Day I Flunked Out of Air Traffic Control School." *Air & Space Smithsonian*, May 2014. Accessed February 8, 2019. https://www.airspacemag.com/history-of-flight/ flights-fancy-May-2014-180950132/.

Dettmer, Jamie. "Drug Trafficking is a Family Affair." *Washington Times*, April 8,1997. Accessed February 8, 2019. http://www.rave.ca/en/ news_info/198000/all/.

"Doña Ana County Commissioners Hearing: Lomas del Poleo & Binational Development (video transcript), February 26, 2008.

Driver, Alice. *More or Less Dead*. Tucson, AZ: University of Arizona Press, 2015.

"El Papa ora ante la tumba de Samuel Ruiz." *Excelsior*, February 15, 2016. Accessed February 8, 2019. https://www.excelsior.com.mx/ nacional/2016/02/15/1075308.

"Emiliano Zapata" *Biography*. Accessed February 7, 2019. www. biography.com/people/emiliano-zapata-9540356.

Erasmus. "A New Sort of Religious Radical." *Economist*, August 20, 2014. Accessed February 8, 2019. https://www.economist.com/ erasmus/2014/08/20/a-new-sort-of-religious-radical.

Faux, Jeff. *The Global Class War*. Washington, DC: Economic Policy Institute, 2006.

Friedman, Anna Felicity. *The World Atlas of Tattoos*. New Haven, CT: Yale University Press, 2015.

Gibler, John. "Fight on the Border." *Z Magazine*, April 27, 2009. Accessed February 8, 2019. https://zcomm.org/zmagazine/fight-on-the-border-by-john-gibler/.

Gilot, Louie. "Rebel Leader Decries Planned Wall, Criticizes Bush, Fox." *El Paso Times*, January 5, 2007.

González, Aureliano Baz. "What is a Maquiladora?" University of Delaware. Accessed February 8, 2019. http://www1.udel.edu/leipzig/texts2/vox128.htm.

González, Juan. "The Assassination of Digna Ochoa: A Look at the Life and Death of the Renowned Mexican Human Rights Lawyer." *Democracy Now!* April 27, 2006. Accessed February 8, 2019. https://www.democracynow.org/2006/4/27/the_assassination_of_digna_ochoa_a.

Goodman, Amy. "'We Made a Devil's Bargain': Fmr. President Clinton Apologizes for Trade Policies that Destroyed Haitian Rice Farming." *Democracy Now!* April 1, 2010.

Harvey, Neil. "Cross-Border Alliance Protests Juárez Evictions." *Grassroots Press*, January 27, 2008.

———. "Foxconn Development Raises Stakes for Lomas de Poleo." *Newspaper Tree*, August 22, 2008.

Hernández, Alan. "Pope Francis Tells Mexico's Indigenous Peoples: 'Sorry Brothers.'" *Vice News*, February 15, 2016. Accessed February 8, 2019. https://news.vice.com/en_us/article/mbnxdp/pope-francis-tells-mexicos-indigenous-peoples-sorry-brothers.

Hernandez, Daniel. "The Art Outlaws of East L.A." *L.A. Weekly*, June 6, 2007. Accessed February 8, 2019. https://www.laweekly.com/news/the-art-outlaws-of-east-la-2149157.

Hooks, Christopher. "Q&A with Molly Molloy: The Story of the Juarez Femicides Is a 'Myth.'" *Texas Observer*, January 9, 2014. Accessed February 8, 2019. https://www.texasobserver.org/qa-molly-molloy-story-juarez-femicides-myth/.

Horwath, Justin, and Joey Peters. "Well, Well." *Santa Fe Reporter*, July 30, 2013. Accessed February 8, 2019. https://www.sfreporter.com/news/2013/07/30/well-well/.

Hudgins, Matt. "Baseball Stadium Bolsters El Paso's Resurgence." *New York Times*, May 28, 2013. Accessed February 8, 2019. https://www.nytimes.com/2013/05/29/realestate/commercial/in-el-paso-out-with-the-old-city-hall-in-with-a-new-stadium.html.

Ibárruri, Dolores. "La Pasionaria's Farewell Address." *Modern American Poetry*, November 1, 1938. Accessed February 8, 2019. http://www.english.illinois.edu/maps/scw/farewell.htm.

Karlin, Mark. "The Border Wall: The Last Stand at Making the US a White Gated Community." *Truthout*, March 11, 2012. Accessed February 8, 2019. https://truthout.org/articles/the-border-wall-the-last-stand-at-making-the-us-a-white-gated-community/.

Kennis, Andrew. "A Tale of Two Cities: Ciudad Juarez and El Paso." *Truthout*, May 4, 2012. Accessed February 8, 2019. https://truthout.org/articles/a-tale-of-two-cities-ciudad-juarez-and-el-paso/.

Kilpatrick, Kate. "In Juarez, Vigilante Justice Comes in a Blond Wig." *Al Jazeera America*, November 20, 2013. Accessed February 8, 2019. http://america.aljazeera.com/articles/2013/11/20/in-juarez-vigilantejusticeinablondwig.html.

Lauria, Carlos. "Mexican Cartels Keep Up Social Media Intimidation." Committee to Protect Journalists. Accessed February 8, 2019. https://cpj.org/blog/2011/11/mexican-cartels-press-social-media-intimidation-ca.php.

Le Texier, Emmanuelle. "L'Opération Gatekeeper à la frontière entre Mexique et Etats-Unis: le nouveau mur de Berlin?" *Amnesty International*, May 20, 2003.

"Leonardo Boff." *Liberation Theologies*. Accessed February 8, 2019. https://liberationtheology.org/people-organizations/leonardo-boff/.

Light, John. "Free Trade's Trojan Horse." *Sierra*, November–December 2016. Accessed February 8, 2019. https://www.sierraclub.org/sierra/2016-6-november-december/feature/free-trades-trojan-horse.

Liu, Kat. "NAFTA and Immigration," *Inspired Faith, Effective Action*, October 18, 2010. Accessed February 8, 2019. http://socialjustice.blogs.uua.org/immigration/nafta-and-immigration/.

Llenas, Bryan. "Mexican Journalists Who Live Under Threat from Drug Cartels Take Paris Attack Personally." *Fox News*, January 9, 2015. Accessed February 8, 2019. https://www.foxnews.com/world/mexican-journalists-who-live-under-threat-from-drug-cartels-take-paris-attack-personally.

Luckey, Peter. "Can You Sing Mary's Song?" A sermon delivered at U.C.C. Plymouth Church, Lawrence, KS, October 2, 2011.

Lyderson, Kari. "Development and the Desert: Border Land Struggle Turns Bloody in Ciudad Juarez, Mexico." *Upside Down World*, August 28, 2008. Accessed February 8, 2019. http://upsidedownworld.org/archives/mexico/development-and-the-desert-border-land-struggle-turns-bloody-in-ciudad-juarez-mexico/.

Mariarte, "Alerta: A War Without Uniforms." *Borderfotos* 16, January 8, 2008.

Martinez Prado, Juan Carlos. "Lomas de Poleo: Un campo de concentración en la frontera." *Vanguardia, MX*, January 21, 2011. Accessed February 8, 2019. https://vanguardia.com.mx/lomasdepo leouncampodeconcentracionenlafrontera-634805.html.

McAlpine, John. "The Homicide of Digna Ochoa." *Advocate* 60, no. 3, May 2002. Accessed February 8, 2019. https://www.lrwc.org/ the-homicide-of-digna-ochoa/.

McConahay, Mary Jo. *Maya Roads*. Chicago: Chicago Review Press, 2011.

McDermott, Jeremy, and Steven Dudley. "MS13." *Insight Crime*, November 16, 2015.

McGahan, Jason. "To Kill a Journalist." *Texas Observer*, January 24, 2013. Accessed February 8, 2019. https://www.texasobserver.org/ to-kill-a-journalist/.

Mendoza, Louis. "The Same on Both Sides of the Border." *Twin Cities Daily Planet*, December 6, 2007. Accessed February 8, 2019. https:// www.tcdailyplanet.net/same-both-sides-border/.

"Mexico's Zapatista Rebel Movement Marks 20 Years," *USA Today*, January 2, 2014. Accessed February 8, 2019. https:// www.usatoday.com/story/news/world/2014/01/02/ mexicos-zapatista-rebel-movement-marks-20-years/4284461/.

Miroff, Nick. "Mass Kidnapping of Students in Iguala, Mexico, Brings Outrage and Protests." *Washington Post*, October 11, 2014. Accessed February 8, 2019. https://wapo.st/2SHxkiI.

Missionary Society of St. Columban, "From Lapsed Catholic to Catholic Missionary." *Columban Fathers*. Unavailable February 8, 2019. www.columban.org/content/view/36/78/.

Morton, Bill. "Update on Lomas del Poleo (Agrarian Court in Chihuahua)." *Grassroots Press*, January 10, 2009.

———. "Updates on Lomas del Poleo: Assault and Another Legal Delay." *Grassroots Press*, July 6, 2009.

Muñoz, Gloria Ramirez. "Los de Abajo," *La Jornada*, March 22, 2008. Accessed February 8, 2019. https://www.jornada.com. mx/2018/10/27/opinion/01601pol.

Murphy, James. *The Martyrdom of Saint Toribio Romo*, Liguori, MO: Liguori Publications, 2007.

Nathan, Debbie. "The Best Laid Plan." *Texas Monthly*, February 2013. Accessed February 8, 2019. https://www.texasmonthly.com/ articles/the-best-laid-plan/.

———. "Making a Killing: Land Deals and Girl Deaths on the U.S.-Mexico Border." *Newspaper Tree*, January 4, 2008.

Neikirk, William. "Reich: Labor 'Plain Wrong' on Nafta." *Chicago Tribune*, July 14, 1993. Accessed February 8, 2019. https://www.chicagotribune.com/news/ct-xpm-1993-07-14-9307140084-story.html.

New Mexico Office of the State Engineer. "Water Rights Reporting System (NMWRRS)." Accessed February 8, 2019. http://www.ose.state.nm.us/WRAB/index.php.

Ortiz, Mónica Uribe. "Low Water Deliveries from Mexico Hurt Texas Farmers." *KJZZ 91.5*, August 28, 2013. Accessed February 8, 2019. https://kjzz.org/content/8936/low-water-deliveries-mexico-hurt-texas-farmers.

Paley, Dawn. "Corn on the Border—NAFTA and Food in Mexico." *Watershed Sentinel*, March 7, 2013. Accessed February 8, 2019. https://watershedsentinel.ca/articles/corn-on-the-border-nafta-food-in-mexico/.

Pastrana, Daniela. "Permanent People's Tribunal Sets Up Shop in Mexico." *Inter Press Service*, October 25, 2011. Accessed February 8, 2019. http://www.ipsnews.net/2011/10/permanent-peoples-tribunal-sets-up-shop-in-mexico/.

Patel, Raj. *Stuffed And Starved: The Hidden Battle for the World Food System*. Brooklyn, NY: Melville House, 2007.

Paterson, Kent. "Juarez Femicides Trial Verdict: Milestone or Miscarriage of Justice?" *Americas Program*, July 21, 2015. Accessed February 8, 2019. https://www.americas.org/juarez-femicide-trial-verdict-milestone-or-miscarriage-of-justice/.

———. "The Mexican State Goes on Trial in Ciudad Juarez." *Frontera NorteSur*, May 30, 2012. Accessed February 9, 2019. https://fnsnews.nmsu.edu/the-mexican-state-goes-on-trial-in-ciudad-juarez/.

Puente, Arturo González. "Water Economics in the Conchos River, Chihuahua, Irrigation Districts, 1990–2001." *Research Gate*, October 2002. Accessed February 8, 2019. https://www.researchgate.net/publication/303347503_Water_Economics_in_the_Conchos_River_Chihuahua_Irrigation_Districts_1990-2001.

"A Q&A with David Dorado Romo." *Texas Monthly*, November 2010. Accessed February 8, 2019. https://www.texasmonthly.com/articles/a-qa-with-david-dorado-romo/.

Ramos, Javier Garza. "Being a Journalist in Mexico is Getting Even More Dangerous." *Washington Post*, February 18, 2016. Accessed February 8, 2019. https://www.washingtonpost.com/posteverything/wp/2016/02/18/being-a-journalist-in-mexico-is-getting-even-more-dangerous/.

La Redacción, "El Diego, jefe de La Línea, ordenó matar al periodista Armando Rodríguez: PGR." *Almargen*, November 13, 2014. Accessed February 8, 2019. http://almargen.mx/el-diego-jefe-de-la-linea-ordeno-matar-al-periodista-armando-rodriguez-pgr/.

Reich, Robert. "Hillary and Barack, Afta Nafta," February 29, 2008. Accessed February 8, 2019. http://robertreich.org/post/257309371.

Rhodes, Ron. "Christian Revolution in Latin America: The Changing Face of Liberation Theology." *CRI*, 2015. Accessed February 8, 2019. http://www.equip.org/PDF/DL100-1.pdf.

Rice, Andrew. "Life on the Line." *New York Times*, July 28, 2011. Accessed February 11, 2019. https://nyti.ms/2DsIGNT.

Robert F. Kennedy Center for Justice & Human Rights. *Digna Ochoa*. Unavailable February 11, 2019. rfkcenter.org/digna-ochoa.

Rodríguez, Teresa. *Las Hijas de Juárez*. New York: Atria Books, 2007.

Romeo, Raul. "A Brief History of the Zapatista Army of National Liberation." *ROAR Magazine*, January 1, 2014. Accessed February 8, 2019. https://roarmag.org/essays/brief-history-ezln-uprising/.

Roper, Kelly. "Mexican Prison Tattoos." *LoveToKnow*, nd. Accessed February 8, 2019. https://tattoos.lovetoknow.com/Mexican_Prison_Tattoos.

Ross, John. *The War Against Oblivion: The Zapatista Chronicles*. Monroe, ME: Common Courage Press, 2002.

San Martin, Ines. "Pope Francis Apologizes for Exploitation of Native Peoples, Calls for Economic Justice." *Crux*, July 9, 2015. Accessed February 8, 2019. https://cruxnow.com/church/2015/07/09/pope-francis-apologizes-for-exploitation-of-native-peoples-calls-for-economic-justice/.

Semple, Kirk. "Mexico Ready to Play the Corn Card in Trade Talks." *New York Times*, April 2, 2017. Accessed February 8, 2019. https://www.nytimes.com/2017/04/02/world/americas/mexico-corn-nafta-trade.html.

———. "Missing Mexican Students Suffered a Night of 'Terror,' Investigators Say." *New York Times*, April 24, 2016. Accessed February 8, 2019. https://www.nytimes.com/2016/04/25/world/americas/missing-mexican-students-suffered-a-night-of-terror-investigators-say.html.

Sirota, David. "The Regrets of Bill Clinton." *Salon*, April 23, 2010. Accessed February 8, 2019. https://www.salon.com/2010/04/24/bill_clinton_s_contrition/.

Solotaroff, Paul. "Who Stole the Water?" *Men's Journal*, July 2014. Accessed February 9, 2019. https://www.mensjournal.com/features/who-stole-the-water-20140623/.

Stokes, Benjamin, and Ryan Menezes. "6 Terrifying Things You Learn as an Air Traffic Controller." *Cracked*, February 9, 2015. Accessed February 8, 2019. http://www.cracked.com/personal-experiences-1656-6-terrifying-things-you-learn-as-air-traffic-controller.html.

Subcomandante Insurgentes Marcos. *The Other Campaign: la otra campaña*. San Francisco, CA: City Lights Publishers, 2008.

Thomas, J. Matthew. "The World Hands Project: Anapra, Mexico." *Forward AIA*, 2009.

Tuckman, Jo. "Jane Fonda Leads March to Force Action against Mexican City's Women-Killers." *Guardian*, February 16, 2004. Accessed February 8, 2019. https://www.theguardian.com/world/2004/feb/16/gender.mexico.

Weaver, Thomas. "Mapping the Policy Terrain: Political Economy, Policy, Environment and Forestry Production in Northern Mexico." *Journal of Political Ecology* 3, no. 1 (1996). Accessed February 8, 2019. https://journals.uair.arizona.edu/index.php/JPE/article/view/20458.

Weisbrot, Mark. "NAFTA: 20 Years of Regret for Mexico," *Guardian*, January 4, 2014. Accessed February 8, 2019. https://www.theguardian.com/commentisfree/2014/jan/04/nafta-20-years-mexico-regret.

Welsome, Eileen. "Eminent Disaster." *Texas Observer*, May 4, 2007. Accessed February 8, 2019. https://www.texasobserver.org/2483-eminent-disaster-a-cabal-of-politicians-and-profiteers-targets-an-el-paso-barrio/.

———. "Lomas Del Poleo," December 27, 2007. Accessed February 8, 2019. http://www.eileenwelsome.com/lomas-del-poleo/.

"Who Governs Chihuahua?" *El Enemigo Común*, October 6, 2008. Accessed February 8, 2019. https://elenemigocomun.net/2008/10/who-governs-chihuahua/.

Williams, Jon. "Development through Displacement: The Creation of a New Export Processing Zone on the U.S.-Mexico Border." Master's Thesis, New Mexico State University. 2010.

Wines, Michael. "Drought Shrivels Rio Grande, Altering a Region." *Houston Chronicle*, April 12, 2015. Accessed February 8, 2019. https://www.houstonchronicle.com/news/houston-texas/texas/article/Drought-shrivels-Rio-Grande-altering-a-region-6195435.php.

"Zapatista Leader Address Bridge Crowd." *El Paso Times*, November 1, 2006.

ABOUT PM PRESS

PM Press was founded at the end of 2007 by a small collection of folks with decades of publishing, media, and organizing experience. PM Press co-conspirators have published and distributed hundreds of books, pamphlets, CDs, and DVDs. Members of PM have founded enduring book fairs, spearheaded victorious tenant organizing campaigns, and worked closely with bookstores, academic conferences, and even rock bands to deliver political and challenging ideas to all walks of life. We're old enough to know what we're doing and young enough to know what's at stake.

We seek to create radical and stimulating fiction and nonfiction books, pamphlets, T-shirts, visual and audio materials to entertain, educate, and inspire you. We aim to distribute these through every available channel with every available technology—whether that means you are seeing anarchist classics at our bookfair stalls, reading our latest vegan cookbook at the café, downloading geeky fiction e-books, or digging new music and timely videos from our website.

PM Press is always on the lookout for talented and skilled volunteers, artists, activists, and writers to work with. If you have a great idea for a project or can contribute in some way, please get in touch.

PM Press
PO Box 23912
Oakland, CA 94623
www.pmpress.org

PM Press in Europe
europe@pmpress.org
www.pmpress.org.uk

FRIENDS OF PM PRESS

These are indisputably momentous times—the financial system is melting down globally and the Empire is stumbling. Now more than ever there is a vital need for radical ideas.

In the years since its founding—and on a mere shoestring—PM Press has risen to the formidable challenge of publishing and distributing knowledge and entertainment for the struggles ahead. With over 300 releases to date, we have published an impressive and stimulating array of literature, art, music, politics, and culture. Using every available medium, we've succeeded in connecting those hungry for ideas and information to those putting them into practice.

Friends of PM allows you to directly help impact, amplify, and revitalize the discourse and actions of radical writers, filmmakers, and artists. It provides us with a stable foundation from which we can build upon our early successes and provides a much-needed subsidy for the materials that can't necessarily pay their own way. You can help make that happen—and receive every new title automatically delivered to your door once a month—by joining as a Friend of PM Press. And, we'll throw in a free T-shirt when you sign up.

Here are your options:

- **$30 a month** Get all books and pamphlets plus 50% discount on all webstore purchases

- **$40 a month** Get all PM Press releases (including CDs and DVDs) plus 50% discount on all webstore purchases

- **$100 a month** Superstar—Everything plus PM merchandise, free downloads, and 50% discount on all webstore purchases

For those who can't afford $30 or more a month, we have **Sustainer Rates** at $15, $10 and $5. Sustainers get a free PM Press T-shirt and a 50% discount on all purchases from our website.

Your Visa or Mastercard will be billed once a month, until you tell us to stop. Or until our efforts succeed in bringing the revolution around. Or the financial meltdown of Capital makes plastic redundant. Whichever comes first.

Abundance

Michael Fine

ISBN: 978-1-62963-644-3
$17.95   352 pages

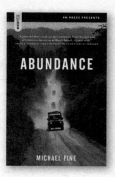

Julia is an American medical doctor fleeing her
own privileged background to find a new life
delivering health care to African villages, where
her skills can make a difference. Carl is also an
American, whose very different experiences
as a black man in the United States have
driven him into exile in West Africa, where he is an international NGO
expat. The two come together as colleagues (and then more) as Liberia
is gripped in a brutal civil war. Child soldiers kidnap Julia on a remote
jungle road, and Carl is evacuated against his will by U.S. Marines. Back
in the United States he finds Julia's mentor, Levin, a Rhode Island MD
whose Sixties idealism has been hijacked by history. Then they meet the
thief. Then they meet the smuggler. And the dangerous work of finding
and rescuing Julia begins.

An unforgettable thriller grounded in real events.

"Michael Fine's novel, Abundance, *is a riveting, suspenseful tale of love,
violence, adventure, idealism, sometimes-comic cynicism, class conflict and
crime . . . a story that displays both the deep disconnect between the First
and Third Worlds and our commonalities."*
—Robert Whitcomb, former finance editor of the *International Herald
Tribune* and former editorial page editor of the *Providence Journal*

*"Michael Fine takes us into the heart of a country at war with itself. But our
journey, in battered Land Rovers, along potholed red dirt roads, is propelled
by love, not hate. That love offers hope for Liberia, our often forgotten sister
country, and anyone who confronts despair. Read* Abundance. *Reignite your
own search for a life worth living."*
—Martha Bebinger, WBUR

*"A powerful first novel—an epic stretching from the civil wars of Liberia to
the streets of Rhode Island. A joy to read!"*
—Paul J. Stekler, Emmy-winning documentary filmmaker

Damnificados

JJ Amaworo Wilson

ISBN: 978-1-62963-117-2
$15.95   288 pages

Damnificados is loosely based on the real-life occupation of a half-completed skyscraper in Caracas, Venezuela, the Tower of David. In this fictional version, six hundred "damnificados"—vagabonds and misfits—take over an abandoned urban tower and set up a community complete with schools, stores, beauty salons, bakeries, and a rag-tag defensive militia. Their always heroic (and often hilarious) struggle for survival and dignity pits them against corrupt police, the brutal military, and the tyrannical "owners."

Taking place in an unnamed country at an unspecified time, the novel has elements of magical realism: avenging wolves, biblical floods, massacres involving multilingual ghosts, arrow showers falling to the tune of Beethoven's Ninth, and a trash truck acting as a Trojan horse. The ghosts and miracles woven into the narrative are part of a richly imagined world in which the laws of nature are constantly stretched and the past is always present.

"Should be read by every politician and rich bastard and then force-fed to them—literally, page by page."
—Jimmy Santiago Baca, author of *A Place to Stand*

"Two-headed beasts, biblical floods, dragonflies to the rescue—magical realism threads through this authentic and compelling struggle of men and women—the damnificados—to make a home for themselves against all odds. Into this modern, urban, politically familiar landscape of the 'have-nots' versus the 'haves,' Amaworo Wilson introduces archetypes of hope and redemption that are also deeply familiar—true love, vision quests, the hero's journey, even the remote possibility of a happy ending. These characters, this place, this dream will stay with you long after you've put this book down."
—Sharman Apt Russell, author of *Hunger*

Fire on the Mountain

Terry Bisson
with an introduction
by Mumia Abu-Jamal

ISBN: 978-1-60486-087-0
$15.95   208 pages

It's 1959 in socialist Virginia. The Deep South
is an independent Black nation called Nova
Africa. The second Mars expedition is about
to touch down on the red planet. And a
pregnant scientist is climbing the Blue Ridge in search of her great-great
grandfather, a teenage slave who fought with John Brown and Harriet
Tubman's guerrilla army.

Long unavailable in the US, published in France as Nova Africa, *Fire on
the Mountain* is the story of what might have happened if John Brown's
raid on Harper's Ferry had succeeded—and the Civil War had been
started not by the slave owners but the abolitionists.

*"History revisioned, turned inside out . . . Bisson's wild and wonderful
imagination has taken some strange turns to arrive at such a destination."*
—Madison Smartt Bell, Anisfield-Wolf Award winner and author of
Devil's Dream

*"You don't forget Bisson's characters, even well after you've finished his
books. His* Fire on the Mountain *does for the Civil War what Philip K. Dick's*
The Man in the High Castle *did for World War Two."*
—George Alec Effinger, winner of the Hugo and Nebula awards for
Shrödinger's Kitten, and author of the Marîd Audran trilogy.

*"A talent for evoking the joyful, vertiginous experiences of a world at
fundamental turning points."*
—Publishers Weekly

"Few works have moved me as deeply, as thoroughly, as Terry Bisson's Fire
On The Mountain *. . . With this single poignant story, Bisson molds a world
as sweet as banana cream pies, and as briny as hot tears."*
—Mumia Abu-Jamal, prisoner and author of *Live From Death Row*, from
the Introduction.

Clandestine Occupations: An Imaginary History

Diana Block

ISBN: 978-1-62963-121-9
$16.95   256 pages

A radical activist, Luba Gold, makes the difficult decision to go underground to support the Puerto Rican independence movement. When Luba's collective is targeted by an FBI sting, she escapes with her baby but leaves behind a sensitive envelope that is being safeguarded by a friend. When the FBI come looking for Luba, the friend must decide whether to cooperate in the search for the woman she loves. Ten years later, when Luba emerges from clandestinity, she discovers that the FBI sting was orchestrated by another activist friend who had become an FBI informant. In the changed era of the 1990s, Luba must decide whether to forgive the woman who betrayed her.

Told from the points of view of five different women who cross paths with Luba over four decades, *Clandestine Occupations* explores the difficult decisions that activists confront about the boundaries of legality and speculates about the scope of clandestine action in the future. It is a thought-provoking reflection on the risks and sacrifices of political activism as well as the damaging reverberations of disaffection and cynicism.

"Clandestine Occupations *is a triumph of passion and force. A number of memoirs and other nonfiction works by revolutionaries from the 1970s and '80s, including one by Block herself, have given us partial pictures of what a committed life, sometimes lived underground, was like. But there are times when only fiction can really take us there. A marvelous novel that moves beyond all preconceived categories.*"
—Margaret Randall, author of *Che on My Mind*

"*Diana Block creates a vivid and engaging tapestry of how political passion interweaves with the intricacies of personal relationships.* Clandestine Occupations *takes us into the thoughts and feelings of six different women as each, in her own way, grapples with choices about how to live and act in a world rife with oppression but also brightened by rays of humanity and hope.*"
—David Gilbert, political prisoner, author of *Love and Struggle*

Autonomy Is in Our Hearts: Zapatista Autonomous Government through the Lens of the Tsotsil Language

Dylan Eldredge Fitzwater
with a Foreword by John P. Clark

ISBN: 978-1-62963-580-4
$19.95   224 pages

Following the Zapatista uprising on New Year's Day 1994, the EZLN communities of Chiapas began the slow process of creating a system of autonomous government that would bring their call for freedom, justice, and democracy from word to reality. *Autonomy Is in Our Hearts* analyzes this long and arduous process on its own terms, using the conceptual language of Tsotsil, a Mayan language indigenous to the highland Zapatista communities of Chiapas.

The words "Freedom," "Justice," and "Democracy" emblazoned on the Zapatista flags are only approximations of the aspirations articulated in the six indigenous languages spoken by the Zapatista communities. They are rough translations of concepts such as *ichbail ta muk'* or "mutual recognition and respect among equal persons or peoples," *a'mtel* or "collective work done for the good of a community" and *lekil kuxlejal* or "the life that is good for everyone." *Autonomy Is in Our Hearts* provides a fresh perspective on the Zapatistas and a deep engagement with the daily realities of Zapatista autonomous government. Simultaneously an exposition of Tsotsil philosophy and a detailed account of Zapatista governance structures, this book is an indispensable commentary on the Zapatista movement of today.

"This is a refreshing book. Written with the humility of the learner, or the absence of the arrogant knower, the Zapatista dictum to 'command obeying' becomes to 'know learning.'"
—Marisol de la Cadena, author of *Earth Beings: Ecologies of Practice across Andean Worlds*

Diario De Oaxaca:
A Sketchbook Journal of Two Years in Mexico

Peter Kuper, with an introduction
by Martín Solares

ISBN: 978-1-60486-071-9
$29.95   208 pages

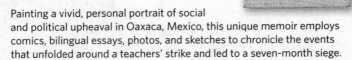

Painting a vivid, personal portrait of social
and political upheaval in Oaxaca, Mexico, this unique memoir employs
comics, bilingual essays, photos, and sketches to chronicle the events
that unfolded around a teachers' strike and led to a seven-month siege.

When award-winning cartoonist Peter Kuper and his wife and daughter
moved to the beautiful 16th-century colonial town of Oaxaca in
2006, they planned to spend a quiet year or two enjoying a different
culture and taking a break from the U.S. political climate under the
Bush administration. What they hadn't counted on was landing in the
epicenter of Mexico's biggest political struggle in recent years. Timely
and compelling, this extraordinary firsthand account presents a distinct
artistic vision of Oaxacan life, from explorations of the beauty of the
environment to graphic portrayals of the fight between strikers and
government troops that left more than 20 people dead, including
American journalist Brad Will.

*"Kuper is a colossus; I have been in awe of him for over 20 years. Teachers
and students everywhere take heart: Kuper has in these pages born witness
to our seemingly endless struggle to educate and to be educated in the
face of institutions that really don't give a damn. In this ruined age we need
Kuper's unsparing compassionate visionary artistry like we need hope."*
—Junot Díaz, Pulitzer Prize winning author of *The Brief Wondrous Life of
Oscar Wao*

*"Peter Kuper is undoubtedly the modern master whose work has refined the
socially relevant comic to the highest point yet achieved."*
—Newsarama

"An artist at the top of his form."
—Publisher's Weekly

Teaching Rebellion: Stories from the Grassroots Mobilization in Oaxaca

Edited by Diana Denham
and the C.A.S.A. Collective

ISBN: 978-1-60486-032-0
$21.99   384 pages

In 2006, Oaxaca, Mexico came alive with a broad and diverse movement that captivated the nation and earned the admiration of communities organizing for social justice around the world. What began as a teachers' strike demanding more resources for education quickly turned into a massive movement that demanded direct, participatory democracy. Hundreds of thousands of Oaxacans raised their voices against the abuses of the state government. They participated in marches of up to 800,000 people, occupied government buildings, took over radio stations, called for statewide labor and hunger strikes, held sit-ins, reclaimed spaces for public art and created altars for assassinated activists in public spaces. Despite the fierce repression that the movement faced—with hundreds arbitrarily detained, tortured, forced into hiding, or murdered by the state and federal forces and paramilitary death squads—people were determined to make their voices heard. Accompanied by photography and political art, *Teaching Rebellion* is a compilation of testimonies from longtime organizers, teachers, students, housewives, religious leaders, union members, schoolchildren, indigenous community activists, artists, journalists, and many others who participated in what became the Popular Assembly of the Peoples of Oaxaca. This is a chance to listen directly to those invested in and affected by what quickly became one of the most important social uprisings of the 21st century.

"Teaching Rebellion presents an inspiring tapestry of voices from the recent popular uprisings in Oaxaca. The reader is embraced with the cries of anguish and triumph, indignation and overwhelming joy, from the heart of this living rebellion."
—Peter Gelderloos, author of *How Nonviolence Protects the State*

"These remarkable people tell us of the historic teachers' struggle for justice in Oaxaca, Mexico, and of the larger, hemispheric battle of all Indigenous people to end five hundred years of racism and repression."
—Jennifer Harbury, author of *Truth, Torture, and the American Way*

Getting Up for the People: The Visual Revolution of ASAR-Oaxaca

Contributors: ASARO • Mike Graham de La Rosa • Suzanne M. Schadl

ISBN: 978-1-60486-960-6
$19.95   128 pages

Getting Up for the People tells the story of the Assembly of Revolutionary Artists of Oaxaca (ASARO) by remixing their own images and words with curatorial descriptions. Part of a long tradition of socially conscious Mexican art, ASARO gives respect to Mexican national icons; but their themes are also global, entering contemporary debates on issues of corporate greed, genetically modified organisms, violence against women, and abuses of natural resources.

In 2006 ASARO formed as part of a broader social movement, part of which advocated for higher teachers' salaries and access to school supplies. They exercised extralegal means to "get up," displaying their artwork in public spaces. ASARO stands out for their revitalizing remix of collective social action with modern conventions in graffiti, traditional processes in Mexican printmaking, and contemporary communication through social networking. Now they enjoy international recognition as well as state-sanctioned support for their artists' workshops. They use their notoriety to teach Oaxacan youth the importance of publicly expressing and exhibiting their perspectives on the visual landscape.

"The Assembly of Revolutionary Artists of Oaxaca (ASARO) protest and rebel through their art, which follows a tradition established by important Mexican artists of the past including the Mexican Muralists and the Taller de Gráfica Popular. ASARO connects with their artistic and cultural history through a familiar and provocative manner that results in a visual language that is distinctly their own. Getting Up for the People *is a significant contribution to the field of graphic arts history, but more than that, it gives light to the vital work of this important artist collective."*
—Theresa Avila, PhD, author of "Laborious Arts: El Taller de Gráfica Popular & the Meaning of Labor in Las Estampas de la Revolución Mexicana"